SHERLOCK HOLMES

The Langsdale House Mystery

Christopher D. Abbott

Other Titles

MYSTERY: THE DIES SERIES
Sir Laurence Dies
Dr. Chandrix Dies

MYSTERY: THE WATSON CHRONICLES
SHERLOCK HOLMES: A Scandalous Affair
SHERLOCK HOLMES: The Curse of Pharaoh
SHERLOCK HOLMES: The Langsdale House Mystery
SHERLOCK HOLMES: The Black Lantern

FANTASY: THE SONGS OF THE OSIRIAN SERIES
Songs of the Osirian [Book 1]
Rise of the Jackal King [Book 2]
Daughter of Ra [Book 3]
Citadel of Ra [Book 4]
Songs of the Osirian: Companion

SUPERNATURAL/HORROR
Progenitor

ANTHOLOGIES
All That Remains
Beast: A New Beginning
Beast: Revelations

HORROR
Escaping Matilda
Revolting Tales: Christopher D. Abbott & Todd A. Curry

CONTENTS

Other Titles

SHERLOCK HOLMES

The Langsdale House Mystery

Foreword

I have added this story to my chronicles because it presents the reader with an unobstructed view of the unique gifts which my friend, Mr Sherlock Holmes, had in abundance. I have documented many cases in which Holmes showcased his talents, but it would not be an exaggeration to say, certainly in this case, that at this point in our association he had never risen higher. Holmes proved his ingenuity by outwitting those who he considered being possessors of far greater intelligence to that of the common criminal. This was a period where Holmes and I had just developed the bond that would, eventually, outlive him. I look back at those days with fonder memories than I once held. I suspect it is simply the nostalgia of an old man reminiscing on happier times. There is a proverb my friend would often employ: distance lends enchantment to the view. Through the eyes of one as old as I, who now looks back at the adventures we once shared, the distance of time certainly makes it feel enchanting.

The Langsdale House Mystery, unlike A Scandalous Affair, was a far darker business. Murder and conspiracy are not light topics, and the case at Langsdale House touched on subjects I considered utterly repugnant at the time. When I was a younger man, it appalled me at how those in high society could manipulate the law and gloss over their venalities, in a way the ordinary man in the street could never hope to do. This modern time is no exception. One constant always remains.

Time and time again those age-old institutions continually use their power to keep scandal hidden behind the closed doors of their haughty, immoral fortresses. Still, if there was one good thing to come from the sinking of the Titanic, it was to expose the hideous imbalance of class in our country, and lay it into the open for all to see. Perhaps times are changing? The disgust I held for corruption of powerful people, and their institutions, remains as firm today as it did back then, but newer experiences have caused me to re-evaluate the things I used to hold such powerful feelings against. My world is certainly very different now.

The story you are about to read tells a tale set in the backdrop of a time when things were far simpler. I look out of my window onto a world dominated by electricity, motor cars, and fashions, none of which I fully understand. Holmes predicted the evolution that technology would bring us. He said to me, when we were talking about candles, that men like Edison were modernising our world at a rate which defied belief. Holmes always held a childlike excitement for the advance of science. I recall I thought the entire idea fanciful. How wrong I was then, and how terrified by it all I am now.

Let us, then, escape the terrors of 1920s England and travel back to those distinctly uncomplicated times. I invite you to walk with me up the stairs of 221b Baker Street, into the sitting room I miss so dearly. The fire of Mrs Hudson, newly made, must by now be roaring in that old grate. There, we can join my old friend as he employs those amazing observation and deduction skills I have so often recounted. Are you sitting comfortably, dear reader?

Hark! But surely that is the footfall of the Scotland Yarder, Inspector Bradstreet, on our stair? Has he come to recount a mysterious tale that requires the urgent attention of Mr Sherlock Holmes? Why don't we read on to find out...?

John H. Watson, MD (Retd)
8th March, 1924

Chapter One

What possible reason could motivate someone to push a spoonful of jam into a dead man's mouth

I recall from my notes that it was on an extremely cold Saturday evening in early November 1889 when Inspector Bradstreet of Scotland Yard's "B" Division joined us for brandy and cigars, as was his usual habit during that period. My friend entertained a select number of detectives at Baker Street and Bradstreet, being what he considered a step above the rest, was naturally one of them. Those evenings to my mind were rather dull, consisting mainly of notes, reports, and defence documents for those cases Holmes had assisted on, along with lengthy minutia of procedural paperwork for documents needed to be presented in court, which are essential but held little interest for me.

As the night wore on, and the two men continued unaware that I was also in the room, I lost myself in the latest reports from the current Russian influenza pandemic, which was also referred to as the Asiatic flu. Modern transport infrastructure had assisted its spread across Europe in frightening time. I was just reading the spread had reached Vaxholm in Sweden, largely because of the vast amount of traffic that passes through the Baltic shipping routes, when I noticed Bradstreet and Holmes putting their paperwork away. When they joined me at the fire, I poured brandy for us and lit a cigar.

Inspector Bradstreet cradled his brandy bowl loosely in his large hands. Holmes, preferring his long-stemmed pipe over a cigar, lit it and blew out the match. Bradstreet seemed lost in thought for a moment, his eyes on the flickering light of the fire. Holmes's eyes fixed on Bradstreet's, and when they turned on me, I noticed a half smile cross his face.

Holmes took a long pull on his pipe, let out a cloud of blue smoke, then said, 'Why don't you tell us all about it, Bradstreet?'

The inspector, to his credit, didn't act in the least bit surprised.

'That obvious, am I?' he said with a chuckle.

'Something has distracted you the entire evening,' Holmes said with a shrug. 'That much is obvious.'

Bradstreet took a long drink before he answered.

'It's this Langsdale House business,' he finally remarked.

Holmes looked up at me and frowned, then turned his eyes on Bradstreet. 'I'm sorry, Langsdale House business?'

'Yes,' he replied. A look of surprise crossed his brow. 'I'm amazed you haven't heard about it. There was a report today in the Times, although how these reporter fellows get sensitive information like that, I'd really like to know.'

'I've been engaged in some particularly complex chemical analyses for most of the day, I have not had the time to read anything. Tell us about it.'

Bradstreet put down his glass and pulled out a little notebook. 'It was a perplexing affair.'

'The best ones usually are,' Holmes remarked, refilling his pipe.

'I was called by one of my local sergeants, at South Kensington station, to what he described as a grotesque situation in Langsdale House.'

Holmes raised an eyebrow. 'Grotesque?'

'His exact word.'

'Interesting, and the substance of this grotesqueness?'

'A stepfather and stepson murder-suicide.'

'Very succinct,' Holmes remarked. 'Now, give us the details.'

'Langsdale House is near to where Cromwell and Warwick cross, walking distance from Earl's Court. It is a fairly large estate with ten house staff, all of whom, except for the housekeeper and groundsman, live in a detached house on the west side of the property. Langsdale is home to Doctor Wallace Houston-Smythe, his wife Marjorie Houston-Smythe, and her son Harold Houston. There is also a housekeeper, Mrs Harriot Dawson, and her husband the groundsman, Peter Dawson.'

'Is the property too small to house the other domestics?' I asked.

'No, Doctor Watson, it's enormous, and could easily house all the staff with rooms to spare. I thought it a little unusual, to be honest. Actually, the entire house was unusual. The rooms I was permitted to view, specific to the case, were empty of almost all their furniture. You'd think no one lived there at all, given that. When I asked Mrs Dawson about it, she explained moving the staff out was recent and had taken her by surprise.'

Holmes, who'd been slowly circling the tip of his pipe around his lips, said, 'How recent?'

'I should say around three months ago.'

'Did the housekeeper offer any explanation for these moves?'

'Not satisfactorily,' Bradstreet replied. 'It didn't seem pertinent to the investigation so I dropped it. Do you think it's relevant?'

'Well, it is data,' Holmes replied. 'As to its relevance, only time will tell. What is your assessment of the housekeeper?'

'She's a hard Irish lady, Mr Holmes. A lightly tanned woman who might be older than she appears. I'd put her at about forty, but given the way she makes herself up, she could be nearer fifty. She's typical of her Irish blood, doesn't suffer foolish questions nor impertinence. I've dealt with a lot of domestics and she seemed a little below her station.'

'What gave you this impression?'

'It was something in her demeanour. You could easily be mistaken into thinking Mrs Dawson might actually own the place. She's a well-spoken lady. Educated, even. More like a governess than a housekeeper. She certainly doesn't seem to question the motives of her employers. From what I could gather when the move was ordered, she implemented them and didn't seem to care much for why.'

Holmes made a note on his cuff and when he looked up, I detected that little sparkle in his eyes I knew so well. 'What of the husband?'

'Not remotely in her class. He's a ruddy-faced man of around fifty, with grizzled hair and a sour disposition. Has the look and behaviour of a man who drinks heavily. That was clear when I interviewed him. Aside from the odour, he kept throwing furtive looks at his wife. Sometimes his concentration was so poor, she answered for him. There was something a little odd about them both. I couldn't put my finger on it, but since they were not the subject of my investigation, I put those concerns to one side.'

'Were you able to interview the wife?'

'Not immediately. Given the circumstances, she was pretty upset. When Sergeant Birch first arrived with his constables, he said he couldn't get much out of her. He'd only been able to speak to her through the bedroom door, which she had apparently locked herself behind. Getting her to come out was almost impossible. After I had interviewed the housekeeper, I eventually persuaded her to speak with me. She just sat there sobbing behind a heavy black veil. When she found her moments of lucidness, she confirmed what the housekeeper had already told me, almost word for word. Since I could get nothing more from her, I allowed her to retire to her room. A little while later, the housekeeper told me she'd given her a sedative. Quite right too. Poor woman.'

'Well then,' Holmes said, gesturing. 'Let us move to the grotesque circumstances of this apparent murder-suicide.'

'It's all pretty simple, really. Doctor Houston-Smythe had shot and killed his stepson, after an argument between them, then retired to an upstairs room and promptly killed himself.'

'A nasty affair,' I remarked. 'But hardly what I would consider grotesque.'

Holmes appeared to agree, as a look of boredom now replaced his earlier expression of interest.

'Mundane would seem to be a better word choice, I fancy,' he said.

'I agree with you both.' Bradstreet leant forward. 'Sergeant Birch took me to the body of the son, Harold, first. He was a good-looking young man of twenty. We found him slumped backwards in a wooden chair in the centre of an almost empty room. Killed immediately from a bullet through his head. There didn't appear to have been a struggle. We found no weapon and like almost all the other rooms, there was no other furniture, well, except for an empty cupboard, and a small wooden table beside the dead man.' Inspector Bradstreet sat upright. 'Mr Holmes, you'll never guess in a million years what I found on it.'

Holmes raised an eyebrow. 'Since I do not make it a habit to guess, I will wait for you to tell me.'

Bradstreet winked at me. 'There was a jam jar sitting on it,' he said, then sat back into his chair and crossed his arms.

Holmes gave him a blank stare. 'I'm sorry... a jam jar?'

Bradstreet chuckled. 'I know. Strange, isn't it?'

'What was in it?' I asked.

'Blackberry jam, Doctor. It was opened with a good scoop missing. There was also jam on the table and the floor. Here's the other odd thing. When I examined the poor fellow's mouth, it was full of the stuff. He had swallowed none of it as far as I could tell.'

This knocked the bored expression right off Holmes's face. He sat upright, pulling the pipe from his mouth. 'Was there a spoon with it?'

Bradstreet grinned. 'No, Mr Holmes, there wasn't.'

'He used his fingers then?' I interjected.

'Clean,' replied Bradstreet triumphantly.

Holmes sat back in his chair and smoked. He was lost in thought for a minute or two, then he broke from his contemplation and smiled. 'Remarkable, and Doctor Wallace Houston-Smythe?'

'He was a younger man at just forty-three. He was dead in an upstairs room in a similar chair, slumped against a table. As with the son, he died from a bullet to the head, a revolver still clasped in his right hand.'

'Conclusive then. What can you tell me about the room?'

'Empty, Mr Holmes, aside from the table and chair. There was a heavy green candle which appeared to have fallen when he slumped against it. The remarkable thing was, I found—'

'A spoon, perhaps?'

Bradstreet seemed a little crestfallen at my friend's deduction. 'A silver one, yes, but how could you know that?'

Holmes placed a finger against his lips. 'It wasn't an unreasonable supposition. Was there any residue on it?'

Bradstreet grinned. 'It was covered in jam, as was the dead man's left hand and cuff.'

Holmes flashed him a smile. 'How remarkable.'

'What do you make of it?' I asked.

Holmes shrugged. 'I make nothing of it. It is merely data.'

'It's new for me, I'll admit, but I suspect you'll see more in it than I did.'

'Undoubtably,' Holmes remarked.

Bradstreet slapped his knee as he laughed. 'The magic clue that solves everything for you, eh, Mr Holmes?'

Holmes remained unreadable and simply shrugged. 'There is nothing more deceptive than an obvious clue, Bradstreet.'

'I don't disagree, but it is odd, you must admit?'

'I think the word grotesque, in this instance, was particularly well chosen. So, having examined both scenes, what conclusions did you draw?'

Bradstreet frowned. 'Well, none. The case is closed.'

Holmes raised an eyebrow, made a quick look in my

direction, then back to Bradstreet. 'Is it?'

'By decree of the chief inspector. According to the witnesses, the pair were engaged in a ferocious argument. Both the housekeeper and Mrs Houston-Smythe's statements were very clear on that point. Once this argument ended, Doctor Houston-Smythe took a revolver from the gunroom, and shot his stepson with it. Reeling from shock, and terrified, both women say they then heard him go up the stairs. He'd locked himself into a room. A minute or so later, they heard another shot. Chief Inspector Mulgrave ordered me to wrap it all up. I'll admit the jam stuff gave me a reason to question him, along with some other nagging questions that weren't sufficiently cleared up.'

'Such as?'

'A lack of any furniture for a start.'

'Perhaps the domestic staff took it to the new house,' I offered.

Bradstreet didn't look convinced. 'Some of it, maybe, but there were dining rooms with no tables in. Where did they eat?'

'All good questions, and certainly ones to add to our data,' Holmes said. 'Did the two women witness Doctor Houston-Smythe shoot his stepson?'

'No, they were in a separate room. That's where they overheard the argument.'

'I see,' Holmes said. 'And the substance of this argument?'

'They didn't rightly know.'

'I'm sorry,' Holmes said, a look of confusion crossing his hawkish face. 'You said they overheard it.'

'What they recalled were raised voices. The thick walls muffled the actual conversation.'

Holmes seemed satisfied. 'We establish, then, that neither actually witnessed Harold's murder, or Doctor Houston-Smythe's apparent suicide?'

Inspector Bradstreet gave a slight nod.

As Holmes sat in thought, I asked the question I'd really hoped we'd have had an answer for. 'What do you think the jam signifies?'

The inspector shrugged. 'I asked the housekeeper about that, but she had no answers. "Doctor Wallace was not in his right mind," she said. Maybe Harold liked to eat jam? Maybe that caused the argument? Perhaps Doctor Wallace put jam into Harold's mouth because of it. "Why do you think he took the spoon with him?" I asked. "People who lose their minds do strange things," she retorted. I could get nothing more from her.'

'You have no answer of your own?' I persisted.

'No. The whole thing is perplexing.'

'With so many unanswered questions, I find it odd your superiors would consider the case closed, yet perhaps I should not be surprised by it.'

Bradstreet rubbed at his eyes. 'Chief Inspector Mulgrave was satisfied by the witness's recounting of the circumstances, which agreed with the police surgeon's findings. I pointed out several inconsistencies, ones you've already raised, including this jam business. He would hear nothing of it. His tolerance to my questioning only went so far. Following my procedures, I raised it with the superintendent who oversees the Division. He listened to my concerns, looked through my notes, but ultimately agreed with Chief Inspector Mulgrave's conclusions. It left me with little choice in the matter. Mulgrave shut my investigation down and I've since been reassigned. He's scrutinising my every move for attempting to subvert him. I can spend no time on it, but if it interests you...'

Holmes pulled his pipe from his mouth. 'It does, as you knew it would.'

Inspector Bradstreet seemed relieved.

'Do you believe something other than these two deaths has occurred in that house?'

Bradstreet frowned. 'If you mean, do I think my superiors were a little too quick to shut it all down? Then, yes.'

Holmes pointed his pipe at Bradstreet. 'Your instincts could be wrong.'

The inspector smiled. 'And if so, I will not be taking any risks.'

'Ah,' Holmes said. 'Since I am not bound by the politics and procedures of Scotland Yard's hierarchy, your wish is for me to make certain enquiries for you?'

'It can't be anything official.' Bradstreet stood. 'You are not likely to receive much of a welcome.'

Holmes remained thoughtful for a short time.

'How would you recommend I insert myself into a case already deemed closed by the official police?'

'During my investigation, I had time to chat with a few of the domestics. There's a young chambermaid working at the house named Shelly Decker. Her actual name is Patty Smith. I know almost all the regular girls who prostitute in South Kensington, and she's notorious. She recognised me immediately and I put the fear into her. I suspect she thought I would give her away, but sometimes it's better to be owed a favour, if you get my meaning. I'd start with her.'

'You can give me the streets and times she works?'

Bradstreet tore a page from his book and handed it to Holmes. 'There's a few bits of information on that paper that might help.'

Holmes ran his eye over it and then folded it. 'I see. If I should uncover something?'

'Come to me with it. If you discover anything, we'll need to be smart about how we play it.'

Holmes nodded in agreement. 'And the local constabulary?'

'I still have pull there. Speak with Sergeant Birch, he's a good intelligent man. I'll make sure the rest stay out of your way.'

'Forgive my bluntness,' Holmes said, his features unreadable. 'If you have omitted something of value, something you later might regret you did not say, I ask that you tell me now.'

Bradstreet shook his head. 'There is nothing pertinent, but I think you've read some things that will help.'

Holmes's features had hardened. 'And that is to be your last word on the subject?'

'I've told you everything I can. Speak with Sergeant Birch.'

'You know I cannot promise anything.'

Bradstreet smiled. 'I don't require a promise, Mr Holmes, just a new set of eyes.'

'Then you shall have them both.' Holmes remarked, softening his brow.

'And mine too,' I offered. 'If that is acceptable?'

Inspector Bradstreet inclined his head at me, then shook Holmes's hand.

'I had better be going. I have to file these reports at the court first thing. Goodnight, Doctor Watson, and Mr Holmes…' He held his grip on Holmes's hand for a moment longer. 'Thank you.'

I returned from seeing Bradstreet out to find Holmes cradling several books he had pulled from our cabinet. He dropped them onto the floor by the fire and sat down amongst them, spreading them out. I sat opposite and watched as he flicked through the pages. I admit I thought the circumstances in these two deaths to be odd. The case appeared on the balance of the witnesses and evidence to be pretty solid, but there were too many unanswered questions.

'There are difficulties,' Holmes muttered as I raised those questions. 'But then, there are always difficulties. Would you get my "H" index?'

'You think there's more to this affair than a murder suicide?' I said, handing him the volume.

Holmes looked up from the page. 'Oh yes,' he said, and lowered his eyes again to the text. 'There are several points of interest.' He gave an exclamation and closed the book.

'Aside from the jam business, it all seems pretty ordinary, but I dare say I have missed the obvious.'

Holmes gave me a look. 'Does it not strike you as odd that a house large enough to lodge a staff of ten, with rooms to spare, is empty, with those domestics apparently all bottled up in a smaller house some distance away?'

'Maybe they prefer their privacy?'

'And yet they were all moved out three months ago, except for the housekeeper and her husband. Privacy, it would seem, was not an issue previously. If it is so now, then why were only some domestic staff required to vacate the house?'

'Yes, why leave a housekeeper and groundsman?'

'Indeed,' Holmes said as he closed another book and picked up the next in the pile. 'Something occurred three months ago that warranted the house to be emptied. That is where we must focus our efforts.'

'Do your indexes tell you anything about the dead men?'

Holmes shook his head. 'Not the men, no, but Langsdale House has a history, and one perhaps Bradstreet has no prior knowledge of.'

'What history?'

'Something grotesque,' he replied with a wink at me. 'It is not the first time in its two hundred years that blood has been spilt inside its walls.'

I laughed. 'You keep records of old houses now?'

'I do not keep records of old houses, as you say, but where crime occurs in frequencies that cannot be put down to random chance, I make a note of it.' He filled his pipe and lit it. 'In this instance, the Housing Index of '89 lists properties over a century in age, including their owners. Langsdale House was purchased around two years ago by Mrs Marjorie Houston, later Mrs Marjorie Houston-Smythe.'

'The wife owns the house?'

'She owns the entire estate.'

I was thoughtful for a moment. 'What do you make of the jam business? What possible reason could motivate someone to push a spoonful of jam into a dead man's mouth?'

Holmes pulled his pipe from his mouth. His features seemed more hawkish than usual, as his eyes turned on me. 'I have a theory. It is the single most interesting aspect of Bradstreet's story. I would go so far as to say, it is unique. Perfectly unique.'

'And what is this theory?'

Holmes looked up. 'I suspect it was a message for

someone.'

'A message? Do you think Doctor Wallace Houston-Smythe killed his stepson, put jam in his mouth to send a message, then promptly killed himself?'

Holmes raised an eyebrow. 'That is far too fanciful, Watson.'

'It is inexplicable,' I remarked, somewhat irked.

Holmes nodded. 'That is not understating it.'

'There's something odd about all the ages too. The wife in her late fifties, her son twenty, and her husband only forty?'

'Is it odd, or is it you simply find it distasteful?'

'Probably the latter,' I admitted.

Holmes grunted. 'You said you were willing to assist in discovering the answers, but I cannot promise it won't be dangerous work,' Holmes said as he stood and put his pipe on the mantle.

'I know that,' I replied.

'Then I must ask that you put any prejudices you might have aside. If we are to work this case together, it must be with an open mind, even if the things we discover are distasteful to you.'

The request surprised me. I admit I found it hurtful, but I took his meaning. 'I will do my best.'

'Good man. I fancy there may be more to shock you, in the coming days.'

'There's something deeper to this case then?'

Holmes turned his eyes on me. 'Isn't there always?'

'Well, yes, but I meant something connected to Bradstreet. It didn't escape my notice that you saw something he might not have wanted you to see.'

'Ah,' Holmes said, with a genuine look of surprise. 'Your observations about Bradstreet are correct, he is holding something back.'

'That's the element of danger, you suspect?'

'Perhaps.'

'Yet you're willing to take on his case despite the fact he might not be telling you the entire truth?'

Holmes put a hand on my shoulder. 'Bradstreet would never lie to me, not in the way you suggest. We have history and whilst we might not be on the same terms as you and I, there is a certain bond between us. Let us drop this line of enquiry for now.'

I knew Bradstreet had known Holmes for several years, prior to my taking rooms with him, so I let it go. 'Of course.'

'Then I shall bid you a good night,' he said, slipping past me and opening his bedroom door.

'You saw something, in what Bradstreet was saying, something we all missed. Didn't you?'

Holmes then paused and turned his head. 'Your instincts are on fire this evening, Watson.'

'Tell me,' I begged.

Holmes rubbed his tired eyes, then smiled. 'My long-suffering friend, perhaps I should give you something to ponder. Look over your notes and read to me what Bradstreet said about how he found Doctor Houston-Smythe.'

I flicked back through my notebook and found the page. 'Here we are. Dead in an upstairs room, similar chair, slumped against a table. Bullet to the head, revolver clasped in right hand. Empty aside from the table and chair. A fallen heavy green candle, and a spoon covered in jam.'

'As well as on the dead man's left hand and cuff,' Holmes added.

'Yes, that's right.'

'His left hand and cuff, Watson.'

'I don't see…'

'Read it to me again.'

I frowned at my notes for a moment, then saw what he was suggesting. 'Revolver clasped in his right hand.'

'Excellent, and since his left hand and cuff had jam residue upon them, does that not suggest he was possibly left-handed?'

'And if so, left-handed men don't tend to use their right to operate a revolver. But what if someone put the jam on his left hand to throw us off? But since the police case is now closed, they either missed it, or ignored it.'

'As I said,' Holmes remarked, stifling a yawn. 'It is something for you to ponder over. After breakfast, let us see if the two old dogs, that we are, cannot sniff out the mysteries lurking within that grotesque, inexplicable old mansion.'

Chapter Two

I begin to understand the depth of Bradstreet's concern

Breakfast was a quiet affair with only a brief discussion on the case. After coffee and our morning pipes, I retired to perform my toilet, leaving Holmes standing by the mantle reading the Times. It was a little after nine when I had dressed and returned to our sitting room, where I found my friend seated at the bureau writing several telegrams. I poured myself a fresh cup of coffee and waited for him to finish. Holmes finally put down his pen and collected the telegrams he had written, pushing them into his mouse-coloured dressing-gown pocket. He stood and joined me at the table for coffee.

'Do you have a plan?' I asked.

Holmes was absentmindedly slurping his coffee. I could tell his thoughts were being ordered, because he had that characteristic unfocused look which seemed to clear the moment I spoke.

'We will visit the telegraph office first, then pay a visit to Sergeant Birch in South Kensington. If he is as accommodating as Bradstreet suggests, he might allow us to peek at the two dead men.'

Holmes changed from his dressing gown to his frock coat and laid out on the table those items he usually took on a case, pocketing them one by one. I collected my old service revolver from the drawer in the bureau and loaded it. We collected our sticks and hats, and Holmes opened the sitting-room door and ushered me out. Wrapped up in heavy coats and gloves, we soon emerged into the bitterly wintry morning on Baker Street.

It was a bright sunny, almost cloudless day, but that sun held no warmth for us as we made the short walk to the telegraph office. I lit a cigarette and Holmes, having completed his tasks within, shared one with me while we waited for a cab to arrive. It wasn't a long wait. Once we entered, I pulled the heavy rug over our legs for warmth and we settled in for our journey to South Kensington.

The cab driver slowed to a stop, and we alighted at Earl's Court, which was a short distance from the police station. Once inside, Holmes spoke quietly with the constable on duty, who then showed us into the sparsely decorated waiting room that comprised four chairs, and a small table. We stood and waited for several minutes in silence, and when Sergeant Birch finally entered, he extended his hand to my friend.

Sergeant Birch's thick brow and penetrating vibrant grey eyes took in both of us as he indicated for us to sit. He rubbed at his neatly trimmed moustache, which was greying at its edges, and straightened his uniform, which was immaculate. His bearing and deportment suggested he had served in the military.

'Inspector Bradstreet said you'd be by,' he remarked, placing his hands on the small table we all sat around. 'He also explained that discretion was paramount.' It was clear that last statement was directed at me. No one could have failed to miss the distrustful look in his eyes, least of all me. Without taking those eyes from me, Birch asked: 'You can vouch for this gentleman, Mr Holmes?'

'This is my friend and colleague, Doctor Watson, with whom you may be as frank as you would with me.'

'I meant no offence, Doctor,' Sergeant Birch said. I was happy to see the coldness from his eyes disappear. 'This is a delicate situation, as I'm sure you understand?'

'Perfectly,' I assured him. 'And no offense has been taken by your precautions,' I added.

Birch offered me a grateful smile.

Holmes tapped the table with his gloved fingers, and Birch immediately turned to him.

'We both know why I have come here, and time is of the essence. I should like to ask you some questions, Sergeant, if I may?'

'And I will answer, if I am able,' Birch said.

'You have good local knowledge,' Holmes remarked. 'Give us an account of Doctor Wallace Houston-Smythe's history, leaving no detail out, however insignificant it might seem to you.'

'Of course, Mr Holmes. Doctor Wallace Houston-Smythe is, or I should say was, a fairly respected medical gentleman in the town.'

Holmes smiled. 'Yes, thank you. And now perhaps something not of the official line.'

Birch appeared uncomfortable for a moment, then relaxed into a sigh. 'There have been… whispers.'

'Whispers?' Holmes said. 'You may rely on the confidentiality of us both, Sergeant. Again, I implore you, no detail is too small. Tell us all.'

Sergeant Birch gave a tight smile before continuing. 'It seems Wallace might not have been that doctorly, at least that's what I've heard from his fellow practitioners. One even referred to him as a scoundrel, sir. They almost came to blows in the Rose and Crown. Fortunately, I was there to separate them before it got out of hand. It has been said, by locals, Wallace is not a doctor for the likes of you and me. If you get my meaning?'

'I believe I understand,' I said. 'You're suggesting he's a physician for the wealthy?'

'A high-society practitioner?' Holmes remarked, nodding approvingly at me. 'Yes, it certainly fits with what I have discovered about him. Go on, Sergeant.'

'High society? If that's the term you gentlemen like to use, then who am I to discredit it?' Birch turned to me. 'You're a medical doctor, correct?'

'I am.'

'General practitioner?'

Birch impressed me. 'Yes, and surgeon.'

'Military, too, if I'm not mistaken?'

'Correct again,' I said. 'Have you also served?'

'Only in the force, Doctor. Going on forty years. I'm due to retire this year.'

'You have an eye for observation,' Holmes remarked. 'It sets you apart from your peers.'

'Thank you, Mr Holmes. Well, it's a quiet little station and my wants in life are simple. We're not bigwig detectives, but we keep our minds active. Actually, it really has been just a little hobby I've found useful, from time to time, especially when-'

Holmes had allowed Sergeant Birch to wander far enough. 'Yes, yes,' he said, quickly. 'Perhaps we could return to the information relevant to our investigation?'

Birch reddened a little. 'Of course, Mr Holmes. Doctor Wallace Smythe, as he was prior to his marriage, had a chequered past, but not one you'd want to say in open company. There have been several lawsuits over the past year, but convictions never seemed to stick.'

'Malpractices?' I asked.

'Not that any legal council could pin on him, Doctor. Had he been alive you might have found yourself in Queer Street, if you'd said that in public. As you both pointed out, Wallace appeared to only perform medical duties for wealthy people. I suspect those high-society friends of his he made along the way, had some hand in keeping him out of the courts.' Birch leant forward. 'I also heard it suggested that Wallace's speciality was, how shall I put it? To provide medical treatments to important gentleman for conditions they'd never want discussed, not even in private.'

A foul picture of Wallace was forming, one I did not care for at all. 'You mean he treated those with venereal diseases?'

Sergeant Birch gave a quick nod. 'It's a sordid business, Doctor. As far as I understand, it was only for those who had the means to afford it.'

Holmes rubbed his chin. 'Is this idle gossip from townsfolk, or do you have something substantive to back that claim?'

Birch shrugged. 'There's never anything definitive, you understand? I hear a lot of things. Some of it can easily be corroborated, some can't. Given what I know, it didn't take much to work out why all those expensive and privately owned carriages were going up and down the lane to Langsdale House.'

'Indeed. Again, you impress me. I suppose it is too much to hope that you might recognise one or two of the occupants of said carriages?'

'This area is a little more affluent than others and we see our share of expensive broughams. I had my boys keep a log of those that weren't local, if that's of use?'

Holmes looked pleased. 'I realise you cannot simply hand me a copy of that log, but I would like to run an eye over it, if that is possible?'

Birch was thoughtful for a moment. 'Bradstreet said I should give you anything you asked for, within reason, so I'll arrange for you to see it. We keep an eye on those higher-class escort prostitutes as well, ones you won't find on a street corner. I can give you a list if you need it? Several have been seen coming out from Wallace's surgery. There have been other rumours too. It seems Wallace might have performed operations on those girls. The type of operations needed to fix, well… shall we say, certain conditions that unfortunately result from their chosen profession.'

Holmes pulled out his cigarette case and offered it to us. Birch shook his head, and Holmes and I smoked.

'You're suggesting Wallace performed abortive pregnancy surgery, at the house?' Holmes remarked with a look at me. I shook my head. The vileness of the entire situation caused me to remain silent.

'Again, Mr Holmes, it's not something easily provable. These high-society clients, as you put it, don't tell tales on doctors they trust to keep certain confidences to themselves. Rumours are all we have. Some suggest that Wallace had those poor girls under his control. It makes sense, I suppose. What hope would any of them have, in terms of legal recourse, against him? If a rich man gets a local girl pregnant, they aren't likely to let them keep it, are they? Not if they know someone who can just make it all go away.'

'You've had your eye on Wallace for some time, then?' Holmes said.

Sergeant Birch gave Holmes a disarming smile. 'Chief Inspector Mulgrave and I have kept records, but as most of it is gossip and hearsay, it's never been something we could act on. When a rich doctor has resources that give him access to serving legal writs on the police, it puts us under a spotlight. Without evidence and proofs, we couldn't ever make any official claims. We attempted to build a case against him, but the chief inspector's instructions were clear, and all investigations were promptly ceased. It's all immaterial now, but I suspect quite a few people will breathe a sigh of relief when they discover he's no longer with us. I do have one concern though.'

'Which is?'

'If things are as we think,' Sergeant Birch said, 'could there then be powerful people out there with cause to fear what an investigation into his death might reveal?'

Holmes put a finger to his lips. 'It is a reasonable supposition. I begin to understand the depth of Bradstreet's concern. What can you tell me about Harold Houston?'

'Now there was a queer young man, and that's a fact. He was always a bit of a player, in years gone, but it seems he caught some tropical illness that affected his brain. Gave him some form of mental condition, or so his mother let it be known. He had some pretty poor treatment wherever it was, and afterwards it seems he had the mind of a child in a man's body. From all accounts he became a quiet, nervous young man, with little wants of his own. Quite the contrast to his youthful days, so I understand. The general impression was that most people found him harmless, if perhaps a little strange.'

'And how was Wallace's relationship with his wife's son?'

'I've heard it told that the two of them were not on the best of terms. That all seemed to change when Harold came back with his malady. Mrs Houston-Smythe said Wallace stayed with him day and night. Old Dawson suggested it was probably what led her to marry him.'

'Have you seen or heard anything to corroborate any of this?'

Birch shrugged. 'I can tell you that the locals were not shocked to learn that Wallace killed Harold.'

'I see. That is useful to know. Now, what can you tell me about the domestics?'

'Not much, I'm afraid. There's something like eight or nine girls that work for the family who come and go frequently. We know there are a few prostitutes living there. I've always suspected some of them might have come into service because of Wallace's alleged work on them, but again there's no actual proof of that. I'm sorry I can't be more helpful there.'

Holmes nodded. 'Thank you, your information has added much to what I had already suspected. What of the wife?'

'A proper lady. She's a bit of a recluse. We hardly see much of her. She purchased the house and its estate around two years back, before she married Wallace. Her background is almost as shadowy as her husband's. It seems she might have made a fortune abroad, possibly Australia, that's the fashion these days, isn't it? She settled on the purchase of Langsdale House through a solicitor on the high street. It must have cost a king's ransom. I'll give you his name and address, since it'll only require a public record search and will save you some time. The estate is large, with several outbuildings, most of which are so dilapidated you couldn't hope to make them habitable. It's always been a very private estate. The previous owners died in a boating accident in some foreign place and they had no children, so the estate went up for auction. It's surrounded by thick hedgerows that used to be well maintained, but the new groundsman, Dawson, has since let them grow so wild that you can't see the house until you pass right up the lane.'

'Do you know anything about the housekeeper and her husband?'

'Not an awful lot, Mr Holmes. Harriot and Peter Dawson came into service around, five or six months back? Both seem to be good, God-fearing folk, as far as I understand. She's not one for gossip and has seldom been seen out of the house, except on those rare occasions when she visits town – and even then, it's usually only to collect a parcel from the post office, or perhaps medicines from the pharmacy. She keeps to herself, which isn't unusual. He's a drinker, and a heavy one. A regular at the Rose and Crown, off Cromwell, most evenings after eight. To be truthful with you, Mr Holmes, we get a lot of the information we have on the house from Dawson. After he's had a skinful, his tongue wags easily enough. Lord knows how he makes it home.'

'Had either worked in town before taking a post at Langsdale?'

'No, they came from Ireland. Mrs Dawson and Mrs Houston-Smythe are old friends, and when Mrs Dawson finished her post, they packed up and came to live at Langsdale. As housekeepers go, she isn't that thorough. The place was pretty filthy when I was called to the house. There was hardly any furniture, not even in the main dining room. It's a cold house, Mr Holmes. Full of dark corridors and empty rooms. I certainly wouldn't want to live there, and that's a fact.'

'It might have been a happier, cleaner house had they not moved the staff out?' I suggested.

'The conditions those girls live in aren't much better, Doctor. They do at least have warmth and companionship, something I feel Mrs Dawson wouldn't allow had they still been in the main house.'

Holmes stood. 'You have been most helpful, Sergeant. Would it be possible to arrange a viewing of the two bodies?'

Sergeant Birch considered Holmes's request. 'It's possible. The doctor likes to take lunch in Earl's Court. He's usually gone for about an hour. That gives us a small window at just after twelve. Will that be enough time?'

Holmes pulled out and checked his pocket watch. 'We will take what time you can give us. As it is a little before eleven, we have an hour. Might I use what remaining time we have to glance at your records?'

'Of course, Mr Holmes.'

I stood. 'I think I might take in some fresh air, while you do that, if you would both excuse me?'

They each stood. Sergeant Birch offered me a sympathetic smile, and I read much in his eyes. My thoughts on this entire business were in danger of overwhelming me. When I exited the station, I took a satisfying breath of bitter November air.

Chapter Three

I fear my case has now ended in unglamorous fashion

I must have smoked three cigarettes by the time Holmes emerged through the solid oak door of the station. He joined me, lighting one of his own, and smoked in silence for a while beside me. During my solitude, I had allowed some dark thoughts to clear from my mind, and Holmes must have seen this, because he offered me a tight smile.

He lit another cigarette and blew out his match, throwing it out onto the street.

'It must be demonstrably difficult for a medical man to comprehend why another of his profession might take his training along the lines that Doctor Wallace chose,' he said, keeping his eyes on the traffic that moved past us.

'His specialisation is regrettably necessary,' I remarked. 'But do we know for certain his motivation stemmed purely from financial gain? The choice to be a doctor of medicine is not pure whimsy, Holmes. It is a vocation. I should know.'

Holmes inclined his head. 'We still lack all the necessary facts to build a complete picture of your fellow practitioner.'

'And yet, it would appear that Wallace may have caused

more harm than good, especially to those poor girls.'

'As I have said, with a frequency which occasionally annoys you, we must reserve judgements until such times as we know, for certain, just what picture our evidence paints for us. We cannot simply accept Sergeant Birch's word about any of the people we are investigating as fact, but we must not discount it either.'

'You're right, of course.'

In an uncharacteristic display of affection, Holmes gave a light touch to my shoulder.

'You have a good heart, Watson. I may not voice this often, but I sincerely believe you are the embodiment of the kindness your profession espouses. I can think of no other whom I would choose as a lifelong friend.'

Holmes's words warmed my heart. They certainly were unexpected. Still, Holmes was also a master of reading a person too, and he who knew me better than almost anyone else would surely have seen my discomfort as if I wore a placard announcing it.

'There is yet more to discover before we formulate any further theories. Sergeant Birch recommends a visit to the records office of Scotland Yard. He suggested we could find it illuminating.'

'Well, what do you make of that?'

Holmes flicked his cigarette into the road. 'An astute question. What do I make of it? Sergeant Birch is withholding significant information from us. That he needs us to discover it ourselves, is very suggestive. Despite Birch's strength of character, I read the fear behind his eyes.'

'Sergeant Birch is a forty-year veteran of the force. He doesn't strike me as a man who would fear much. What do you think has elicited it, then?'

'The probable cause is who, not what. Your assessment of Birch is, as far as I can determine, perfectly sound. Bradstreet certainly holds him in very high esteem. We are treading dangerous ground by making assessments without all the facts, but given how Sergeant Birch reacted when he mentioned

Chief Inspector Mulgrave, could we not conceivably pin the cause of his anxieties there?'

The outer door of the station opened, and we turned to see Sergeant Birch marching towards us.

'It's a short walk to the morgue,' he said. 'Let us head there now.'

We followed the broad-shouldered sergeant along the road and down a small alleyway which led to the morgue complex. It was a small, unmarked, red-bricked building with a heavy black door. Sergeant Birch unlocked it and ushered us inside. We navigated down a few corridors, and entered the white-tiled sterile environment where we found three bodies, covered by linen, on dull steel tables. Two of those tables positioned together, the other was further apart. Holmes pulled the sheet off the lone body and we both gasped at the poor victim we saw laying on that table. He or she was horribly burnt, almost down to the skeletal structure in some places. With the tissue and muscle mostly burnt away, with only small dense clusters remaining, it suggested exposure to a significant temperature. I ran an expert eye along the torso. The muscle and internal organs were indistinguishable and fused along the exposed rib cage.

'Good grief,' Holmes said, taking his lens and running it over the partially exposed skull. 'Who is this poor fellow?'

Sergeant Birch came between us. 'We're not sure. He came in this morning.'

'She,' I said, looking up.

Holmes flashed me a rare grin, and Sergeant Birch frowned. 'I'm not sure how you could know that, there isn't much to distinguish...'

'And yet,' I said, pointing. 'The partially exposed pelvis should have told you that almost immediately.'

Holmes chuckled and then pulled the linen back over the body. 'One mystery at a time,' he said. 'Let us look at the real prize.'

Birch pulled the linen off the two men, and their

youthfulness struck me. Harold's naked body showed him to be in good shape. His muscular definition and lean physique suggested he had been athletic. There was a gaping hole in his head, which I was expecting to see, but what surprised me was the number of ulcerous skin sores and blemishes that travelled along the arms and chest, down to his stomach. I was about to comment, when Holmes pulled the linen down and began an examination of the poor fellow's groin and genitals, which were covered with clusters of sores. Sergeant Birch turned his back as I came beside my friend. The sickening truth of his condition was not lost on either of us. Holmes stepped back and handed me the glass.

'Take a look,' he said.

I examined the unmistakable cluster of lesions and sores and handed him back his glass. Holmes covered the cadaver's modesty, then pried open the mouth and made yet another detailed examination. The jam Bradstreet mentioned to us was now gone. Only a light residue of it was still visible on the lips, but those blackened and silver-stained teeth and gums told their own story.

I went to offer my thoughts, but Holmes put a finger to his lips and shook his head, indicating Birch – who had his back to us – with a nod. I wasn't sure why he would not want the obvious diagnosis of mercury poisoning said aloud, since the doctor who examined him could surely not have missed it, but I followed his lead.

Holmes gave a loud cough and covered the body. Birch turned and seemed relieved.

'Let us take a peek at the good doctor now,' Holmes said, and pulled the sheet down to expose the man's entire body. Again, Birch turned away, and Holmes and I made a careful examination. A few minutes in, we heard the sounds of footsteps coming our way. Birch hissed at us, and Holmes carefully replaced the linen, and manoeuvred me to the first body we had examined.

A man in a white coat opened the door, followed by a well-dressed ruddy-faced man, with a bushy moustache and beard.

He removed his bowler and stared at us.

'What the devil!' he cried, then gave Sergeant Birch an evil look.

Before anyone could say anything, Holmes stepped forwards and extended his hand.

'It's Chief Inspector Mulgrave, is it not? You might remember me from a case…'

'I know who you are,' Mulgrave said. The sneer on his face seemed permanently etched. 'What I want to know, Mr Holmes, is what are you doing here without the police doctor's permission? You recognise I could have you arrested and charged for your impertinence?' Chief Inspector Mulgrave threw another dangerous look at Birch, who opened his mouth possibly to explain things. He was saved by an interruption from Holmes.

'Hardly that,' Holmes said. 'We are most grateful to Sergeant Birch, who has been helpful in assisting me to identify this poor woman's remains.' He pulled back the linen. 'I fear my case has now ended in unglamorous fashion,' he said with a sigh, 'but since the family have engaged me…'

'We haven't identified her yet, Mr Holmes,' the doctor said, interrupting him. He covering the body with the linen and Holmes stepped away.

Mulgrave rubbed his chin as his eyes remained fixed on Holmes. The suspicion he held was clear.

'How could you know anything about her, since we've released no information?'

'I made enquires with Sergeant Birch. I have been investigating a missing person case for some time, as Inspector Bradstreet can vouch. Sergeant Birch was kind enough to let me know a body of approximately the right height had come in. Naturally, I came to view it. I did not intend to cause any problems and apologise unreservedly if offence has been taken, Chief Inspector.'

Mulgrave waved a hand, and his face took on a less hideous expression.

'I am not interested in your apologies, sir. Neither of you

are permitted here. You will both leave, immediately.'

Holmes inclined his head and again extended his hand, but Mulgrave ignored it and turned to Sergeant Birch. 'You,' he said. 'Show these men out and then have the kindness to wait for me in your office.'

Sergeant Birch showed us the door. Once we were outside, Birch blew out his cheeks.

'Will you be able to deal with Mulgrave?' Holmes asked.

Birch gave a small chuckle. 'Don't concern yourself with the chief inspector,' he said. 'You were quick to come up with that story about the girl. I think he almost believed you. I'll do all I can to reinforce it.'

'You are sure that is nothing more I can do to lessen his wrath on you?'

'Thank you, Mr Holmes, but no. I've had plenty of dealings with Mulgrave over the last forty years. There isn't much he can do to me now, especially as I am shortly to retire.'

'Well then, Sergeant. I thank and bid you good day. Come, Watson.'

Holmes led us out along the main street, and much to my joy, we found a small café where we could get a hot pot of tea and lunch. Holmes pulled out his pipe and filled it, and I sipped at my tea.

'I think we can safely say we have made progress,' Holmes said, blowing a cloud of smoke into the air.

'The boy, Harold, had syphilis,' I remarked. 'It looked to be in an advanced stage.'

'How long would you say?'

'Difficult to know, but given the sores on his chest and arms, I'd gauge maybe three to four months?'

'That was my supposition as well. It answers several questions, does it not?'

I put down my tea and pulled out my notebook. 'It coincides with the staff being moved out.'

Holmes nodded in agreement. 'Along with this story of a tropical illness.'

'Might it also answer why jam was found in his mouth?' I asked.

'I see you have a theory of your own? Your suggestion is that the jam was used to mask the mercury poisoning?'

'Is it possible?'

Holmes ran the tip of his pipe unconsciously around his lip. 'It is certainly a consideration. The treatment of mercury will not always manifest blackened and silvered teeth and gums, but when it does, it cannot be mistaken for anything else. If we theorise someone put jam into his mouth, to disguise his true condition, that raises further questions.'

'But even if that was the case, it would only delay things,' I said, in retrospect. 'They would quickly discover his disease once they prepared his body for the post-mortem.'

Holmes smiled, and his eyes sparkled in the midday sun streaming through our window. 'You are correct. Let us postulate your theory. Harold's malady had begun expressing in an obvious way. A decision is made to remove those domestics living in the house. The reason, perhaps, to conceal his condition and prevent any gossip.'

'It is certainly plausible, as the jam disguised the signs of Harold's condition, at least during Bradstreet's investigation.'

'That's true,' Holmes said. 'Bradstreet would have known instantly what that discolouration of Harold's teeth and gums signified.'

That made sense. 'And I believe he would have told us, had he known it.'

'Again, true.'

'Is it possible that Wallace murdered Harold to mask his illness?'

Holmes inclined his head. 'I have many theories but not enough data to formulate an appropriate answer. Your suggestion, that an attempt was being made to conceal his condition, is a good and highly suggestive one. We know Harold had syphilis. Was Wallace also infected?'

'I saw nothing on Wallace's body to indicate he suffered the same malady, unless he was in an earlier stage.' I thought about that for a moment. 'Of course, only a post-mortem would give us that answer.'

'Agreed,' Holmes said.

'Might we also consider that Wallace put the jam in Harold's mouth as an act of kindness?'

Holmes frowned. 'To save his wife further embarrassment, you mean?'

'Or maybe to save Harold's?'

Holmes considered this. 'Whichever way you view this data, it presents alternative possibilities. We might even infer, from your theory, that Wallace's action had a different meaning to those I originally considered. Certainly, it gives us a new perspective. If, as you suggest, Wallace was attempting to save others the embarrassment of Harold's condition, it adds support to the theory I have been considering, that Wallace is a victim and not a villain.'

I admit that revelation pleased me. 'I would certainly like to think that's true. It is possible he was just performing his doctorly duty after all?'

'We cannot discount it,' Holmes said through a puff of smoke. 'The facts, in so far as we have them, support the hypothesis Wallace was murdered. Until we learn something which discounts it, we follow that line of reasoning. With this being the case, we must consider what motives exist to account for his death.'

'Perhaps we can use the dead woman we saw in the morgue as justification to investigate the domestics on the estate?' I offered.

Holmes grinned. 'We are of the same mind, although I admit I am surprised to hear you voice it.'

'Why? Because it isn't truthful?' I shrugged. 'I'm aware in the past I have berated you for some of your more unconventional methods.'

'Sometimes with good reason,' he replied, chuckling. 'If we are to stay this course, we must be clever about it. We now know Mulgrave has taken an interest in the case, bigger than perhaps Bradstreet suspects. We must also presume our involvement puts us under Mulgrave's scrutiny.'

'But what can he suspect? You were quite convincing and Sergeant Birch said he would reinforce what you said.'

Holmes smoked for a moment. 'Our presence in the morgue, Watson, will have raised sufficient levels of suspicion in the chief inspector's mind. Regardless of how convincing I appeared to be, that supercilious weasel of a man now has good reason to keep an eye on us. When a stubborn man, like Mulgrave, pulls at a thread it is unlikely he will rest, until the entire thing is unwoven. I expect Birch is at this very moment being interrogated. Bradstreet must surely be next?'

I refilled my cup and finally felt warm again.

'Sergeant Birch seems a pretty solid fellow to me. Do you suspect he will give us up?'

'I do not believe so,' Holmes said. 'On balance, it appears we may have an ally in Sergeant Birch. He furnished us with significant amounts of information. Things he did not need to reveal. Things that Bradstreet should have said when I gave him the opportunity.'

I remembered Holmes had seen something he felt Bradstreet had left out of his plea.

'I wonder why?'

Holmes shrugged. 'A simple answer might be he was testing Sergeant Birch's loyalty. Whatever his motivation, we should be cautious. We cannot assume that Birch is on our side, not until we understand the motive behind what he allowed us to know.'

The look of surprise on my face made Holmes chuckle. 'Oh yes,' Holmes said, leaning against the table. 'Sergeant Birch is a player, of that you can be assured.'

'Another reason, perhaps, why Bradstreet left vital information out?'

'Perhaps.'

'Is it a conspiracy?'

Holmes flashed me that brief smile of his – the one I found entrancing and condescending at the same time – and then sat back into his chair and said nothing more.

Our lunch helped reinvigorate my mood. Holmes sat smoking for a time with that dreamy expression I knew meant that I should keep any thoughts I might have to myself. Holmes finally put down his pipe as a boy cleaned away our dishes.

'Would it incommode you to make a return to Baker Street alone?'

His question did not surprise me, as I knew Holmes well enough by now. 'Not in the least.'

'Excellent,' he said, checking his pocket watch. 'There are some calls I wish to make, which I must do in my own little way. I shall return later.'

With the conversation done, Holmes stood and slipped on his coat and gloves. 'I will see you later for dinner.' With a nod, he put on his hat and left. I remained to finish the dregs of the pot of tea.

It was still sunny when I left the café. Despite the cold, I walked rather than take a cab, making my way to Knightsbridge, and an hour later – after I had taken an enjoyable stroll along the paths of Hyde Park – I emerged onto Oxford Street, stopping briefly at the newsagent on the corner of Baker Street. With my supplies in hand, I finally made it to our steps and not long after I was sat happily beside the roaring fire Mrs Hudson had made up whilst we were both out. As if reading my mind, she came in with a pot of tea and afternoon cake. I was as content as any man could be as I sat and read my newspaper.

The Times article on Doctor Wallace's death was small with very little detail, but given what we'd heard from Sergeant Birch, I completely understood why. The exertion of my long walk took its toll on me, and it wasn't long before my eyes got heavy as I stared at the hypnotic crackling fire. The light knock on the door aroused me from my slumber with a surprised jerk. Mrs Hudson soon entered and I could tell by her face she wasn't happy.

'What is it?' I asked.

'There's a woman at the door, Doctor,' she said in that Scottish way which conveyed her disapproval. 'If you can call her that. She wishes to speak with Mr Holmes. I have told her he is unavailable, but she is most insistent, sir. She won't leave.'

'I will speak with the lady,' I said. 'If she is that insistent.'

'She's no lady,' Mrs Hudson retorted, and turned away.

I was left with a feeling of confusion by the sharp way Mrs Hudson had said those words, but when she returned, I understood why.

The woman appeared clutching a small purse tightly to her midsection. Her white knuckled grip on the tattered bag suggested it contained her life's worth. Her filthy white dress, which had probably once been very elegant, was now shabbily misshapen and ill-fitting. Despite her appearance, underneath the grime and poorly applied make-up, I was met with an attractive face and stunning blue eyes that seemed kind. Her involuntary movements suggested a probable drink dependency, or worse. One did not need to be Sherlock Holmes to determine her choice of profession.

'This is Doctor Watson,' Mrs Hudson said in a thicker Scottish accent than she usually employed. 'Mind your manners, young lady, and speak when spoken to.'

'Very grateful I am, Doctor, I'm sure.' Her voice was soft and her Cockney lilt was light.

When I suggested she should come sit by the fire, I thought I noticed Mrs Hudson's eye twitch.

'Thank you, Mrs Hudson,' I said. 'I will take things from here.'

'Very well, Doctor. Would your guest like any refreshment?'

'It's fine, Mrs,' the girl replied. 'I'll take tea and cake, if there's some going?'

'Will you indeed!' Mrs Hudson replied, her cheeks reddening.

'Thank you, Mrs Hudson. Our guest can finish the cake on the table, but a fresh pot of tea will be most welcome.'

'Very good, Doctor.'

Mrs Hudson took the empty pot and walked out, closing the door, leaving us alone.

'I don't think Mrs likes me much,' my guest said, helping herself to the remains of my afternoon cake. 'Can't say as I blame her. She probably don't see many girls like me in a place like this.'

'Girls like you, Miss…?'

'Harry,' she replied. 'That's me name. Well, not a real one mind, but it'll do for you, if that don't cause no offense?'

'None, I assure you, Harry,' I replied. 'Perhaps you'll explain what you wished to say to Mr Holmes? I am his partner, so you can tell me whatever is troubling you and I will convey it to him.'

'Troubling me?' she chuckled. 'No, mister, Doctor, sorry. It was him what told me to come, see?'

I frowned. 'Holmes invited you here?'

'Now then,' she remarked coldly. From her expression it was clear I had inadvertently caused her offense. 'Don't say it like that. I ain't here for them reasons.'

'I apologise, Harry. I did not mean to suggest…'

'Well then,' she huffed. 'Mind you don't. Mr Holmes paid me a sovereign, right? He knows I got all the muck, see?'

'And what muck will a sovereign get him?'

She laughed, then her eyebrows raised. 'In my game, Doctor? About as much as he wants.'

I ignored the obvious innuendo and was about to ask another question, when the door opened and Mrs Hudson arrived with a fresh pot of tea. Harry, as she wanted to be known, surprised me by standing. It was clear she had rudimentary training in service. It certainly eased the sour expression on Mrs Hudson's face, if only slightly.

'Would you like me to pour, Doctor?' Mrs Hudson said, her old eyes trained on Harry.

'It's fine, Mrs,' Harry pronounced, coming alongside her. 'I'll take care of the nice doctor.'

'I bet you will,' muttered Mrs Hudson. She then left us

alone to continue our conversation.

After Harry poured tea, she sat opposite me and began noisily slurping at her cup.

'Can you tell me anything while we wait?' I asked, if only to get a rest from the grating sound of her slurping, which set my teeth on edge. Harry paused and a slow smile spread across her face.

'Sure. If you got a sovereign too?'

'I have no intention of paying for information you've already been paid for,' I replied with a chuckle.

'More's the pity.'

Harry looked up as the clock chimed the quarter hour, and her smile sank. 'He told me to be here at four, sharp. Seems he ain't so good with time reading, is he?' Harry sniffed and went back to her tea, pausing only to ask: 'I don't suppose there's more cake?'

'I think we have agitated Mrs Hudson enough, don't you?'

'That old bird's all right,' she said. 'But I ain't got time to sit here all afternoon, not when I could be out earning a crust. Unless you, you know, want—'

'No, no!' I had no desire to hear the end of that sentence.

'Pity,' she said, raising her cup to her lips. There was a sparkle in her eye that exposed an intelligence I had previously not considered.

Our front door slammed and I inwardly sighed at the sound of Holmes calling out. It seems Mrs Hudson had unsuccessfully attempted to reproach him. Their hushed conversation reached a fevered peak which stopped shortly before he threw open our sitting-room door. Holmes deposited his hat and stick in the stand by the door, then joined us both by the fire.

'Ah, Harry,' he said, rubbing his hands together. 'You have been keeping Watson entertained, I see?'

'Only because you've kept me waiting, again, you fatuous egotist.'

'It could not be helped,' he responded with a smile.

I admit I gaped at her sudden change in dialogue. Gone

was the brashness and uneducated parlance of her class, replaced now by an educated, well-spoken lady.

'Watson don't gawp, there's a good fellow. May I introduce Lady Harmony Brady, a recruit to our cause.'

'Recruit?' She laughed.

'Charmed, my lady,' I said. 'You certainly have the part down well. It completely fooled me.'

'It was a necessary test,' Holmes said, selecting a pipe from his rack. Once he had it filled and lit, he sat next to us both.

'I passed then?' The expression I felt pulling at my face could hardly have been missed by anyone. It is not always easy to keep my agitation in check.

'With flying colours,' Holmes remarked. His wink did little to quash my annoyance. I shook my head and returned to the dregs of my tea.

'Lady Harmony has certain theatrical skills, Watson, that make her a perfect companion. She has been of service several times.'

'I have never seen nor heard of her before now,' I remarked.

'She can speak for herself.'

Harmony turned a kind smile to me. 'I apologise for the deception, Doctor. My background in theatre, amongst other skills, allows me to maintain a living undercover. Hence the creation of Harry.' Harmony looked to Holmes. 'I've yet to hear why it was necessary though.'

Holmes explained the details of our case, and Harmony listened with steadfast attention.

'You understand what is required?'

Harmony nodded, as she put her cup down. 'Pose as a street girl and gain a position at Langsdale House. Once in place, gather as much information as I can, correct?'

'Capital,' he said. 'But be careful. We're playing a dangerous game, you more than us. Don't take any unnecessary risks, do you understand?'

'Perfectly.' Harmony then stood. 'I'm not an idiot, Mr Holmes.'

'But Holmes,' I protested. 'The streets are no place for a lady, no matter how much theatre training she might have.'

Harmony raised her skirts, exposing her left leg. Before I could protest, I noticed a holster attached to her inner thigh.

'I mentioned I had other skills, Doctor. Your concern is appreciated, but unnecessary.'

'Maybe so, but the streets are prowling with dangerous men. The idea of you, well, being taken advantage of just doesn't sit right, armed or otherwise.'

'I haven't survived this long by not observing those risks, Doctor.'

Holmes handed her a small purse. 'This should cover any little expenses you might incur.'

Harmony tested its weight. 'For now.'

With a nod to us both, Harmony made her way to the door and opened it. Before she left, she turned.

'I take it the usual method of communication will suffice, Mr Holmes?'

Holmes nodded, then dismissed her with a wave of his hand and she left. While Holmes refilled his pipe, I went to the window and observed Harmony disappear down the street.

'What an extraordinary woman. She's not just some theatre actress; who is she, really?'

Holmes sat in his chair. 'Lady Harmony has an interesting background, Watson. Her services are not inexpensive, but she is exactly what we need.'

'And you're sure she will be safe?' I still could not shake the thought of her in that precarious environment. Despite her assurance I knew those dangers could be extreme – far more than she might recognise.

Holmes pulled his pipe from his mouth.

'Harmony will be as safe as anyone else in her position. More so, since the profession she is representing typically has watchers, especially where money is concerned. Street girls, especially the lucrative kind, are usually well protected.'

'And yet, there are many prostitutes who've been murdered or mutilated,' I remarked hotly.

'And far more who haven't. I understand your unease,' Holmes remarked with genuine conviction. 'Prostitution is, by its nature, a treacherous game. There are dangers, of course, but then there are always dangers.'

'I wish there was an answer for why the values of chastity and prudence have been disregarded by these poor fallen women.'

Holmes smiled. 'One of the harsh realities of a society who customarily disregards social and economic concerns, leaves those women little choices in that regard. Let us, however, be reminded that Harmony is no more a prostitute than I am a sailor, just because I dressed as one.'

'True. I suppose I just don't like the idea of her taking on those dangers on our behalf.'

'Because she is a woman?' Holmes asked.

'Yes, if you like. Violent men pray on these women in the most vulgar way.'

Holmes leant forward. 'Harmony can take care of herself. Risk is as much a part of her trade as it is mine. Harmony has seen her share of precarious situations under, I might add, similar circumstances and emerged unscathed. Lady Harmony would not elect to undertake such a cause, without thinking through the horrors you are imagining for her. This is her profession, Watson. Do not imagine for a moment I have recruited her on a whim. It is purely a matter of her unique skills, which she has in abundance. We need her, Watson, and there's the truth. Now, let us drop this point of conversation and consider dinner, as I am half starved.'

Chapter Four

Those crumbs led me to deduce you learnt something of vital importance

With supper finished and our evening ahead of us, Holmes disappeared off to his bedroom, coming out as an entirely different man. He had made himself the image of a lower- to middle-class man, in a grubby dark brown suit and matching bowler. His heavy red moustache and beard matched the tufts of hair I could see haphazardly poking from beneath his tatty brown hat. He searched around for some items to fill his pockets with, then once he was ready, he lit a cigarette and stood smoking by the fire.

'You're going to Langsdale House?' I asked.

Holmes shook his head. 'To the Rose and Crown, Watson.'

'Ah.' I understood now. 'It's a little after seven, you might even make it at the same time Mr Dawson does.'

'That is the goal,' he said, filling a pouch with tobacco and a small clay pipe. 'I should have the time I need to observe and possibly question him, before the night is out.'

'Provided he isn't too inebriated by the time you arrive,' I remarked, chuckling.

'There is that to consider,' Holmes replied, matching my humour. 'But I should be able to learn something. Perhaps I may only determine how he gets himself home after a night of drinking? In any event, I shall be late back and it is unlikely you will see me until morning.'

That wasn't unusual. 'Since you do not need me tonight, I might call on Billings and play a few games of billiards at my club. He has a finger on the medical elite. I might see if he has information on Wallace.'

'An excellent idea, Watson. I wish you a successful night, then.'

'And I you,' I said.

The red-bearded Holmes quietly left and I went upstairs to my room to dress.

It was about an hour later when I readied my attire for the evening. I was preparing to leave for my club, when Mrs Hudson knocked on the door. She came in carrying that customary silver tray upon which she presented a client's calling card. I admit my heart dropped at the sight. Since Holmes was not here to accept whoever it was, I took the card and read it.

'Mr Henry J Popplewick,' I said with a frown. The name seemed familiar.

'He's a younger man, Doctor. I told him I did not believe Mr Holmes was available; as I did not see that red-bearded ruffian who left an hour ago come in by the front door, I assume it was Mr Holmes?'

'Yes indeed.'

She chuckled. 'I shall ask him to return another day, as you're ready for your club.'

I was tempted to agree, but thought better of it.

'No, I can see him. It could be important.'

'Very well. Perhaps he'll have a clue? I'll send him up.'

A few moments later Mr Henry Popplewick entered the sitting room respectfully carrying his bowler.

'Doctor Watson?' he asked, extending his hand to me.

After our greeting, I directed him to the chairs by the fire, and we sat.

'I'm sorry to bother you at this late hour.' Popplewick turned his bowler around by its rim as he spoke. 'I was hoping to catch Mr Holmes.'

'I am afraid Holmes is engaged. Sorry but I cannot say for certain when he will be available. Is there anything I can do to help?'

'For God's sake, please help me. It's Elsie,' he blurted out. 'She's gone missing and I think something dreadful might have happened.' Mr Popplewick sat back in his chair and held a hand to his face, overcome with emotion. I got up and poured some brandy, handing one to him. He took a grateful sip which strengthened him. For several minutes, young Popplewick sat staring into the brandy bowl, lost. He then took another sip, sighed, and wiped his eyes with the back of his hand.

'Sorry. You must think me rather foolish.'

'Not at all,' I replied. The boy seemed heartbroken. I could not help but feel pity for him. 'Why don't you tell me what you can? Who is Elsie?'

'Miss Elsie Palmer. She's my girl. Elsie recently accepted my proposal to marry. She's not had a peaceful life. Elsie was a street urchin after she left the orphanage. When we met, there was an instant attraction. From that moment we spent all our time together.'

'Why don't you tell me a little about yourself?'

'I work at the family grocers in Covent Garden,' he said. 'You might have heard of us, Popplewick and Son?'

I had indeed. 'Of course, who hasn't?'

'Well, after a month I took Elsie home to meet Dad. He's been a widower for ten years after Mum died. When I told him I had met a girl, he seemed very pleased. As soon as he set eyes on my Elsie, he gave a great laugh and was very sweet on her. Called her a fine young lady. Truthfully, I was initially alarmed at his reaction. I wondered if he might almost have been a bit taken with her himself. Elsie is a few years my senior, you understand.'

'How old is she?'

'Thirty, or near about.'

'How did Elsie respond to your father?'

I noticed a slight frown. 'There was a little oddness, at first. Elsie, who can chatter, would hardly speak when he was around, and only then when answering questions. She seemed intimidated by old Dad, but whatever the problem was, they resolved it. Soon after she became quite chatty with him too. It has made living together at the house very easy.'

'You all live together?'

'It's a good arrangement. Elsie has her own room. Dad was insistent upon that.'

'Understandable. Your father approved of the match then?'

Young Mr Popplewick sank back in his chair.

'Well now, here's the thing I don't quite understand. I thought so, but when I broached the subject of marriage, Dad flew into a rage. I have never seen him like this before. It startled me. Dad made it very clear I was not to entertain marrying her. After that, he was dreadfully unkind. Elsie took the brunt of it. It got to a point where said she could no longer stay at the house. I was miserable, as you might understand.'

'Did he give any reason why he was against your union?'

'No,' he replied. 'Dad just forbade me marrying her and said the subject was closed. I thought things might have changed three weeks back, because out of the blue he asked why I didn't bring Elsie around anymore. I told him I thought her unwelcome. Dad shook his head and said she was always welcome. I'll admit he had me confused, but also delighted, as he seemed to have softened on the idea of my marrying her. When I told him, he didn't get angry like before, he just reiterated there were no circumstances under which I could marry a girl like Elsie. I found my voice and told him I wouldn't have those choices made for me. Dad just gave me an evil look. He said if I pursued it, he'd kick me onto the street and out of the family business. I had to assume he meant my inheritance too. I dropped the subject. It was maybe a week later when he asked again when I would bring Elsie back home. Dad's position on marriage hadn't changed. It's all bizarre. How could I do as he asked, with him behaving so unreasonably?'

'It seems peculiar,' I said. 'Has your father acted this way before?'

Popplewick's face reddened. 'I am just twenty, Doctor. Elsie is the first girl who I've had the thought to marry.'

I wondered how I had missed his youthful innocence.

'Elsie is your first relationship, then?'

'She is,' he replied. His dreamy expression further betraying his youth. 'We have been together for a little over three months.'

Three months. Why that timeframe seemed important, I could not put my finger on.

'What can you tell me about Elsie?'

'She works as a maid for a family in a large house in South Kensington.'

I stiffened but held my composure, the importance of that timeframe now clear. I suppressed the excitement threatening to overwhelming me.

'Would that be Langsdale House?'

Young Mr Popplewick gawped at me. I could now appreciate for myself the shocked expression of a client because of a deduction. I had not, however, handled asking with any care, since his highly expressive face turned unreadable, and his eyes narrowed.

'How could you know that?' No one could fail to miss the accusatorial suspicion in his inexperienced eyes.

'I was just reading this,' I remarked, nonchalantly picking up yesterday's paper. 'There's an article that mentioned Langsdale House. You said South Kensington and it immediately brought that house to mind. Was I right?'

It seemed my quick thinking might have saved me any further explanation, for his expression visibly relaxed.

'What an amazing coincidence,' he said. 'Yes, that's the place she works, or I should say worked, since that old bird housekeeper told me Elsie hadn't shown for work and they'd dismissed her. When I questioned her, she threatened to call the law. A few days later, I visited the police to file a report of her missing. The sergeant I spoke with wasn't too helpful. He didn't seem to take me seriously. I've searched everywhere I can think of, Doctor, but she's nowhere. Dad says she up and left probably to save me from embarrassing the family.'

With his emotional state agitated again, he drank a little more of his brandy.

'How long has she been missing?' I asked.

'Five days now,' he said with a miserable sigh.

'And Elsie has no family of any kind?'

'None that I know of.'

'No one whom she might have visited with and perhaps lost track of the days?' I persisted.

'You're sounding like that sergeant,' he said, and again he let out a sigh.

'Sorry,' I remarked with conviction I truly meant. 'These questions must seem ridiculous, but are necessary for the process of an investigation.'

His eyes brightened. 'Mr Holmes will take my case then?'

'I will do all I can to ensure he does. Now, we should make a full account for him.'

I went to my bureau and took out a notepad and pencil. Holmes, I knew, would want as much information as it was possible for me to get. I went through all the details again with Mr Popplewick. When we finished and he had been assured I would present Holmes with all the information, Mr Popplewick left. I looked up as the clock struck ten and realised it was too late to go to my club. My night, however, was neither lost nor wasted. There was now a direct link through Popplewick and Elsie to Langsdale House. I had also found a client for whom Holmes could now legitimately begin an investigation for.

Holmes had not returned by the time midnight had come and gone. Exhausted, I climbed into bed and soon fell into a sound sleep. I awoke the following morning after eight and performed my toilet. Dressed, I entered our sitting room and found Holmes smoking his morning pipe and drinking coffee at the dining room table. He looked up from the Times and smiled as I came beside him. He dropped his paper on the table as I sat.

'I see you did not go out to your club last night.'

I poured myself a coffee and sat opposite him. 'And how did you determine that?'

'It is elementary. The purse you take your money in remains locked in the bureau. It has been your habit for many years to return it only after you have drawn a sufficient replacement for what you spent, from the bank. Since you did not get up early and visit the bank, it requires small guile to conclude you did not, in fact, go to your club.'

'You are quite right,' I said.

He eyed me through the smoke drifting from his morning pipe.

'You instead entertained a visitor that has, in your opinion, an important connection to our case.'

I looked up in shock.

'Now come on, Holmes, how could you possibly deduce that?'

'It amazes me you are still surprised by my observations. Something made you change your plans. Since you are a creature of habit, logically, the answer must be, you had a visitor.'

'True, but to determine my visitor's relationship to the case? That's a stretch, is it not? What was the inexplicable clue that told you that?'

Holmes held a sparkle in his eyes. 'It was the crumbs.'

'Crumbs?' I frowned. 'What crumbs?'

'The crumbs you sprinkled over your chair when you brushed them from your jacket. Those crumbs led me to deduce you learnt something of importance. It caused you to break a daily habit, one you have not broken for possibly a year.'

'I admit it's all true,' I said, refilling my cup. 'But from crumbs? You really are a wizard.'

'Hardly,' he said, chuckling. 'It is simply a matter of cause to effect. The crumbs came from a certain biscuit, one you only eat when consuming coffee. You have explained, frequently, that you avoid coffee after five as it causes you to sleep poorly. Breaking this habit was a choice, and from that choice I deduce you were attempting to remain awake. Since I was out, it was not unreasonable to conclude you were awaiting my return. The information learnt then, could only have applied to the case. After your visitor left, you drank coffee and smoked one of your favourite cigars. I conjectured you were waiting to consult me. Since I did not find a note, I concluded what you had to say you deemed too important for a scribble.'

'How do you know we didn't drink coffee and smoke together?' I asked, smugly.

He pointed to the side table.

'I suppose it is possible that you both drank from the same cup? Now, as you have already admitted it was all true, why don't you tell me about it?'

There was no getting away from it. I shook my head and laughed.

'You are a genius,' I said. 'I think you will be quite pleased with me once I explain the circumstances of Mr Popplewick's visit.'

I detailed the events of the night before and read through the notes Mr Popplewick and I had written. He listened while smoking and when I finished my explanation, Holmes stood and went to the mantle to refill his pipe. Once he had it lit, he turned and extinguished the match.

'It is your opinion I should investigate Elsie Palmer's disappearance?'

'Indeed. The coincidence of this young woman's place of employment must surely...'

'I regret, Watson. I cannot take up this case.'

His refusal dumbfounded me. 'What... but why?'

Holmes sighed. 'Consider what we know. A young man,

infatuated with an older woman of whom he knows practically nothing, presents her to a father who seems at first happy, probably that his son has finally sown his oats, but balks at the idea he should marry her. That he allows this woman to remain in his house, in a separate room, surely adds credence to the idea he wishes his son to continue to gain certain life experiences?' He then looked directly at me. 'The separate bedroom might also indicate possibilities which, I stress, would seem utterly repugnant to your more sensitive nature.'

'In what way?'

'Are you sure you want me to explain it?'

I honestly could not grasp what he was trying to tell me. 'Yes, please.'

'I propose Elsie is not her actual name, and she is almost certainly a prostitute.'

That news shocked me. 'How can you make that determination?'

'From the way the father responded. Did he not say, there were no circumstances under which he would allow his son to marry a girl like Elsie? His constant flip-flop between his anger at his son's union with the girl, and an almost obsessive desire she should continue to visit the house, is perhaps, more than suggestive.'

'Meaning what, exactly?'

Holmes raised his eyebrows. 'Given what I have explained, consider why a father would allow a woman to live in his house in a separate room to his son.'

'It's only proper,' I said.

'Your naivety surprises me,' he retorted.

'You mean, the father was also…'

'Quite so.'

The images crossing my mind turned my stomach.

'I suppose it might be as you suggest…'

'Of course, it is,' he said, smiling. 'If I were to think kindly of this Elsie, I might say that her maturity recognised the boy's infatuation had overridden his sense, and she desired to save him any further embarrassment, as the father suggested. The more probable reason was that when she discovered there was nothing to gain from pursuing the young man, as was made clear by the father's threat of disinheritance, she disengaged and moved on to another.'

'Yet she is missing and under circumstances that might be considered suspicious,' I attempted.

'We cannot know that for certain.'

'In any event,' I offered, feeling the strength of my argument slipping away. 'It would lend you a legitimate reason to investigate Langsdale House?'

Holmes seemed to consider this. 'It is the one thing in its favour. But no, it will be a fruitless endeavour. Once the housekeeper confirms Elsie's dismissal for her failure to attend work, which she must surely do by the first question, then we will lose any reason for a continued investigation. Unless there is some evidence of violence, the investigation will surely come to an abrupt end, along with it, any hope of solving our case.'

'What do you mean?'

'I have confirmed Chief Inspector Mulgrave has me under surveillance.'

'There is a genuine prospect this woman's plight might connect with the case at hand.'

'I don't doubt it,' he responded quickly.

There was hope then, and I felt some light at the end of the tunnel. 'Given that, you must agree that investigating her disappearance could lead to answers for both cases?'

Holmes shook his head. 'I cannot agree to that.'

'But,' I retorted in exasperation. 'I made a promise.'

'Then unmake it.'

'I will do no such thing.' I felt my cheeks reddening. Sometimes, I remained bafflingly bewildered by Holmes, the cold, hard reasoner. 'If you will not help Mr Popplewick, then I will.'

'I advise against it,' Holmes said.

'Why? To save you hard work?' I regretted my heated retort the moment it fell from my lips.

'No, my dear friend,' he said, the note of annoyance in his

voice unmistakable. 'To save you from yourself.'

'I apologise.'

We sat in silence for a minute or two. Holmes grunted, and I looked up to his half smile.

'I shall ask Harmony to make enquiries. Will that satisfy you?'

Holmes's casual dismissal of poor Mr Popplewick was disappointing, but I had to admit his solution, as abhorrent as it seemed, rang true. His offer made me feel a little better.

'Yes, thank you.'

Holmes softened his features. 'This boy's lost love cannot dominate our investigation. Are we agreed?'

'Yes, you are right, of course.'

'Then we can put the matter to rest?'

'Indeed. Perhaps,' I added, 'Harmony will discover something?'

'One can only hope. Now, after we have consumed this splendid breakfast that I see Mrs Hudson has worked so hard on, I will tell you what I discovered at the Rose and Crown last night.'

Chapter Five

Good fortune had nothing to do with it, I can assure you

'It was easy to find the right people to join in with,' Holmes said, as he pushed away his empty plate. We moved to the chairs by the fire, where Holmes took his long-stemmed pipe from the mantle, filled and lit it, then continued his story.

'I arrived at the Rose and Crown a little earlier than he, and therefore easily inserted myself into a group of locals who were playing a game of dominos. These men took me as one of their own and it was not long before they were treating me as if we had all been comrades for years. They were quick of tongue and had a lot of tales about Langsdale House. It has a reputation, and not always a pretty one. After we consumed another round of drinks, those tongues soon loosened. The subject of the deaths came up. Each had their own theory, one more fanciful than the next. Still, some of what they said about the goings-on at Langsdale agreed with what we had already learnt. These were tradesmen of one sort or another, and each had, in some capacity, visited the house. It was easy to learn something of substance from each, but not all of it was useful.

'As I have often said, the best source of gossip in a small

town is always the local public house. This proved to be no exception. After dropping a sovereign on the counter, I found the landlord, a rather unimaginative fellow named Gerald Drake, the most helpful. He explained Langsdale was once owned by the family Hodgkin-Tramwell. They lived there through several generations. Drake explained his father was butler to Cecil and Clara Hodgkin-Tramwell, the last members of the family to live at Langsdale House. He told me he would have taken that position, too, had they not both perished abroad. They had no children, which might account for why they travelled so extensively. According to Drake, Cecil and Clara favoured the Americas, where they spent several months out of the year.

'Old families have offshoots, Watson, and this one was no exception. After their deaths, a search uncovered several relatives who'd settled years earlier in America. The landlord could tell me little about them, save they had no interest in returning to England. At the inquest, a verdict of accidental death was reached, and that was when the estate details were laid bare. Over the course of twenty years, several debts had been placed on the estate. There was little choice but to sell it, to satisfy those creditors. After the inquest they dismissed the staff with the estate put up for auction. From what Drake explained, it was around six months later that the estate was purchased by Marjorie Houston. She took residence soon after.'

'Was she the buyer?'

Holmes shrugged. 'Marjorie Houston owns the estate. She either purchased it, or someone purchased it for her. I can corroborate neither scenario. Since sales of this nature are public record, I was able to discover it sold for a third of its value.'

'Considering what Sergeant Birch said, about the lack of furniture and the dilapidated state of the outer buildings and so on, perhaps she is not as wealthy as people assume?'

'I am inclined to agree. Marjorie Houston has hardly any background that I could discover, and hardly anyone has seen her, despite the fact she has been living there for several years. This, as you can appreciate, has created many rumours. She came from America, and not Australia, as Birch suggested.'

'That can't be a coincidence,' I remarked.

'No, and it answers the lingering questions in my mind. But there is more to learn before we look into that.' Holmes smoked for a moment, allowing me to finish my notes.

'Perhaps an hour had passed when I heard the heavy oak door open and in came Dawson. He was as Sergeant Birch detailed. His ruddy complexion and yellowing skin told of years of drinking and those years have not been kind to him either. At a glance he might appear sixty, but is in fact no older than fifty. A shifty untrusting man, who shuffles as he walks, suggesting there may be an underlying lameness in one or both his legs.

'When he settled with his beer, he joined us at our table and we fell into a merry game. Dawson is so used to drink that hardly any man could outdo him. He consumed beer at a rate of four-to-one against my companions and I. It was only after he had relieved himself and returned that his jolly mood seemed to sour. He sat back in his chair and gave a great sigh.

'Bobby Wilkins, a young trainee tailor who works for AG Broker's in the high street, asked him what the trouble was. Dawson complained about several things, but specifically about an old boiler which I gather desperately needed repair. Wilkins continued the conversation for a while, and we all listened. At length, the conversation turned from heating issues to other domestic complaints. At no point during these conversations was there any mention of the two men who had recently died. Since it was the only topic of conversation prior to his arrival, it struck me as odd no one raised it.

'Wilkins then pointed at me and introduced us. I was a plumber, Wilkins explained, out of work and fallen on hard times. Dawson's attention turned to me and, interestingly, his only concern was my rate of pay.'

'Another sign money might be a concern?'

'It certainly was the only subject that mattered. Once we fixed a price, I agreed to come to the house today, at two, to look over his heating issues. We then continued our games, and he his drinking, until almost midnight.'

'Were you able to discover anything of value regarding the two dead men?'

'Fragments of new information are added to the data, but as yet I do not have enough to form an opinion. I did, however, discover how Dawson makes it home after such a heavy night. The landlord has his teenage boy drive him in his cart.'

I chuckled. 'You're going back in disguise to look at the plumbing, then?'

'We are going,' he said, standing.

I raised an eyebrow. 'I am to be in disguise with you?'

'With minor adjustments, here and there, we can definitely make a plumber's mate out of you. We shall have lunch at the Rose and Crown then head to the house.'

The idea of investigating in disguise was, I admit, a little outside of my comfort. Holmes assured me it was necessary, since in order to maintain the pretence of him being a plumber, he would need a partner. So, for the next few hours Holmes got into his disguise and soon afterwards helped with mine. Thankfully, Holmes decided it was not important to give me much in the way of makeup.

Holmes went through my wardrobe, pulling out items of older clothing, which he took away, returning them back in a state under normal circumstances I would never have considered wearing. After a few light touches of colour were added to my hair and eyebrows, he went through a detailed description of the character I was to personify. Perhaps an hour later, once everything was set between us, we set off once more to South Kensington.

*

It was around noon when we sat at the bar in the Rose and Crown. Holmes, who had cultivated a good relationship with

Drake the landlord in a small amount of time, procured the services of his teenage son to drive us to the house. After we finished our lunch, we were on our way.

The rickety cart, which had certainly seen better days, took us to the house along a long lane heavy with unkept brush and bramble overgrowth. Our first glimpse of Langsdale House came as it emerged through a break in the hedges. From a distance, the enormous mansion seemed resplendent, but once we turned onto the drive and left the untamed privets behind, a closer inspection revealed the sad truth that Langsdale House was, in actuality, in significant need of repair. Holmes, who'd said nothing during our journey, shuffled up to the boy and pointed. Our cart came to a stop, and it deposited us at a side entrance where a shuffling, wheezing man, the groundsman Dawson, came to meet us.

Holmes energetically jumped down, taking the bag of tools from me, and greeted Dawson in a handshake. He cheerfully introduced me in a voice I would never have recognised.

'This is my mate, Charlie,' he said.

Dawson reluctantly shook my hand. 'If you'll follow me, I'll show you the problem.'

With no further preamble, Dawson walked towards the door.

We entered the small dark corridor that led to a room cluttered with building materials, following him to the far wall where a freestanding cast-iron boiler with its black japanned finish and bronze plating sat, partially encased in bricks that were crumbled and old. It had probably been an expensive purchase. Its neglected state matched the poor condition of the house. Several pipe coils, mounted on the wall, went along the skirting and up through the ceiling to the floor above.

'We can get it going, no issue, but it won't heat the rooms up right. Sometimes, the radiators don't heat at all. Can you fix it?'

Holmes took out a candle and lit it, examining the boiler and pipes meticulously. After a moment, he returned to us and sighed.

'The problem's not here,' he said. 'I'll have to look at each room that don't heat.'

Dawson gave a furtive look.

'Is that going to be a problem?' Holmes asked.

'I should think not, but stay here while I make sure it's fine.' Dawson then left us and Holmes and I stepped out into the chilly day and smoked.

I followed Holmes further away from the side entrance, his eyes constantly searching the house as I spoke. 'What do we know about plumbing? We'll surely be undone once any work starts?'

'Calm yourself,' he said. 'The basic system of heating requires heat-producing apparatuses, or boilers, a means of distributing the heat via pipes, and heat emitters in the spaces it serves. How difficult can it be?'

I should have known better. Holmes, it seemed, could now add plumbing to his ever-growing list of possible future occupations.

'What is the plan, then?'

Holmes returned to the doorway and lit another cigarette.

'I am confident I can fix the issue,' he said in a hushed tone. 'It also allows for an examination of the house, and specifically, those rooms in which each man died.'

'How will we gain access to these rooms?'

'Via a not-so-obvious ploy,' he offered, winking at me. 'I am sure I will come up with a solution.'

'We are fortunate that the boiler failed and gave us that opportunity.'

Holmes's eyes sparkled under his heavy red brow. 'Good fortune had nothing to do with it, I can assure you.'

Before I could vocalise any surprise, he put a finger to his lips.

'No more questions until we are clear.'

Holmes scuttled to a pair of rubbish bins and began routing through them. As I approached, I could see he was studying several screwed-up papers. With a grunt often associated with his having triumphed, he shoved them into his pocket and led me back inside, where we settled by the boiler. Moments later, the now red-faced Dawson returned.

'We may visit the rooms above, but we must not spend too long doing so,' he intoned rather grumpily. 'The lady of the house is… unwell, and would prefer it if tradespeople weren't traipsing throughout the place.'

Holmes, giving the shaky groundskeeper his best crooked smile, collected his tool bag and met him at the inner doorway.

'Let's see if we can't track this problem down sharp, then.'

Dawson led us through to a back stair which ascended into an untidy kitchen. Holmes, who did not appear to notice its unkept and neglected state, followed the pipes, occasionally marking them with chalk and using a ball of string to take measurements. As I knew nothing about plumbing, I took the notes he dictated. I admit half of what he said made little sense to me. Once satisfied, Holmes picked up his bag and moved on. Dawson shuffled along behind us.

That was how it went for the next thirty minutes. Holmes examined the pipes, along with any radiators, and dictated his odd little notes. We found smaller rooms stacked with boxes and old furniture, and it was obvious from the dust that no one had disturbed them in a long time.

When we finally reached the front of the house, with its narrow, interconnected passageways and high-ceilinged rooms, I recall how taken aback I was by the lack of any personal items. Bradstreet and Birch both stated the house seemed cold, mostly because of its lack of furniture, but to my mind coldness did not adequately express the sentiment of its emptiness. I could not shake the sense of foreboding depression that emanated from what must have been, at one time, a stunning picture of Edwardian architecture. It was almost as if the house itself was miserable. Looking around, I agreed with Bradstreet's sentiment that it would be easy to assume no one lived there.

Holmes, lost in the character of his plumbing persona, chatted away to Dawson as we made our slow survey. While I shivered at the imagery of the old house, he maintained his repetitive work unaware, continually making those odd observational notes. The route took us into several closed adjoining spaces. Dawson's look of utter boredom seemed permanently etched on his lined and yellowing face.

We had finished eight rooms on the ground floor of the west wing, all of which were empty of even carpeting. By now I also understood the sense of the boredom Dawson continued to exhibit. It then occurred to me we could have the same number of rooms to review on the east side. This did little to decrease the onerous nature of our task. Undercover work, I decided, was not as exciting as I had expected it would be. A further ten minutes had passed when we arrived at a room which we found locked. It was the only room that required a key. I perked up a little. Our route had taken us to the foyer which led to the front door. Could this be the room where Dr Wallace had presumably killed Harold Houston? Holmes's voice broke my train of thought.

'Why's this one locked?' he asked.

Dawson simply shrugged as he unlocked and opened the door.

'Something special in it?' Holmes persisted.

Holmes's questions appeared to annoy him. 'Now, then. You mind your business,' he replied, with an unmistakable touch of menace.

'I meant no offence,' Holmes replied. Dawson entered the room and I noticed Holmes's quick study of the doorway and floor as we passed through. He put down his bag and pulled it open, a frown forming as he pushed the tool around inside.

'Well, that's done it,' he said, with a groan. 'I've only gone and left my plumbers' candle somewhere. It's no good, Charlie, we shall have to go find it.'

I observed Dawson narrowing his eyes ever so slightly, then he shook his head.

'If it's a candle you want, I'll find you one.'

'It must be my one, you see? Can't be a normal one.'

The suspicion on Dawson's face was palpable. 'Why?'

'It's a special candle for plumbing.' He had emptied his bag of nearly all the tools. 'I usually carry two, but I must have left one in my other bag.'

The ruddy-faced Dawson's irritation gave way to a look of resignation. 'Fine, I'll go. Where did you leave it?'

Holmes put the tools back in the bag and rubbed his chin.

'I know I used it by the boiler. I had it in the kitchen. Maybe I left it by the pantry door? I suppose it could be in any of the rooms we just came from. Let me go search, it'll be quicker.'

'No, you stay here. Can't have you wandering the place. I'll find it. Stay in this room,' he warned. 'No wandering, you get me?'

'I can't do nothing without it,' was Holmes's response.

Again, I thought I noticed Dawson narrowing his eyes. He then gave a long sigh.

'What does it look like?'

'It's small, about four inches, white, with a red base and measurements along its side. You can't mistake it. I'm sorry to put you to all that trouble.'

'It's fine.'

With a grumble, the groundsman left us to search and as soon as he was gone from sight, Holmes went into action.

'We have perhaps five minutes,' he said to me. 'Can I ask you to stand here and not move or speak while I make my examination?'

The door had opened onto the left side of an almost empty room we now stood in. I observed a chair and side table pushed up against the right-side wall, along with a heavy wardrobe adjacent to the door which was a foot from the doorway. At the far end, partially obscured by thick green curtains, sat a huge bay window. Holmes opened the curtains to increase the light, and through the opening I glimpsed the unkept front lawn.

Holmes stepped in long strides around the room until he made it to the centre. He dropped to the floor, his lens stuck to his eye, and absorbed as much information as he could.

Holmes briefly scraped at something with a knife he'd produced from his pocket, which he deposited into those little white envelopes of his. Once he'd finished with the floor, he made an examination of the chair. Again, his lens went over every inch. I heard him give a grunt as he bent in to examine the back of the chair. Holmes produced a set of tweezers, and again he put something into another envelope. From my position, it was impossible to see what those items of interest were. Finished now with the chair, he turned his lens to the table.

Movement nearby alerted me to Dawson, who had come from a room further down the corridor. I was about to give Holmes a warning, when I noticed Dawson's shaking head. I relaxed as the groundskeeper disappeared into another room.

Holmes was by now stood by the door examining the lock, then the handle, and everything in between. Finally, he turned to the wardrobe. With the door open, I could now see it was empty of any contents. On the side facing me, nearest the door, a large tapestry hung awkwardly from a heavy brass hook. Holmes lifted it with precision, and his lens travelled from every blemish, mark, and screw hole.

Finally, Holmes dropped to the floor where he shuffled along the wardrobe's base, paying particular attention to the visible space between. At one point he stopped to pull a metal item from underneath, which he scrutinised, then tossed it back under.

Dawson gave an audible cry of triumph nearby. He waved Holmes's lost candle at me as he began shuffling back.

'Holmes,' I hissed in warning. He nodded, as he finished his examinations, and came to stand by me.

'Was your study useful?' I whispered from the side of my mouth.

'My data, at least for Harold's murder, is now complete.'

'You discovered something then?' I asked.

'Almost everything,' he replied. Holmes then greeted Dawson at the door, taking the candle from him with exaggerated gratitude.

With our assessment of the downstairs rooms in the west wing now finished, Dawson took us to an ornate staircase and we ascended. Once we came to the first landing, an austere woman with wire-rimmed thick-lensed glasses, silver hair woven into a tight bun, and a drab sleeveless grey-blue dress over a white buttoned-to-the-neck blouse greeted us. She eyed us with obvious suspicion, but the most severe look she reserved for Mr Dawson. I wondered if she simply disapproved of us, or if her disgusted expression was just for him personally.

'Dawson, why are these men coming up the stairs?' she asked, ignoring us completely. Her thick Irish accent, usually a lyrical sound to my ears, grated harshly.

'You know why, Harriot. There's no need to be' – her withering stare caused him to cast his angry eyes downwards – 'difficult.'

Mrs Dawson turned to Holmes and lifted her head slightly as he stepped forward. To my surprise, and that of Mrs Dawson, he promptly fell over a stair with a shriek, landing at her feet. The poor startled woman took a step back. Holmes's clumsiness was uncharacteristic, and I helped him to stand. He held a look of embarrassment as he mumbled an apology.

'Well, if that little display is anything to go by, it's no wonder we still have no heat.'

'Apologies, ma'am,' Holmes said again, holding his cap loosely in his nervous hands. 'Me mate, Charlie, and me is doing God honest work to get it all fixed, begging your pardon.'

'Really?'

I did not think it would be possible for her to appear any sterner, but she managed it.

'Yet, you've both been here nearly an hour and all you've done is wander from room to room, and played fools on the stair.' The accusatorial tone to her words was clear enough to read. It was obvious she thought we were up to no good. 'What do you have to say to that?'

'We've almost pinned down the problem,' Holmes mumbled.

She snorted. 'I don't see that you've done anything at all. How much longer is it going to take you to fix what, I was told, should be a simple plumbing issue? You are plumbers, are you not?'

'Yes, ma'am.'

'But not efficient ones, eh?' The way she raised her eyebrow suggested her question was rhetorical. 'When will the heat be restored?'

'Soon, I'm sure,' Holmes replied. 'It's not simple to pin down, but once I've checked the pipes and such up here—'

'I don't care for explanations nor excuses,' she said sharply, cutting him off. 'You should be downstairs, fixing the boiler, not traipsing throughout the house. I'm not paying wandering fees, so I'm not.'

'We'll be out of your hair, quicker like, if we could see the rooms what have the issues.'

She stared at him for several seconds. Her eyes narrowed slightly, then with a grimace, she turned to Dawson.

'See that they're quicker about things,' she said. 'I have other tasks needing doing, Dawson. Hurry these men along.'

We stepped aside as she strode past. We watched her go along the corridor to our left where she stopped at a large door. Her eyes found us again, then she knocked once, and disappeared inside.

Holmes blew out his cheeks. 'She's a tough old bird, ain't she?'

Dawson, the sting of her rebuff still clear in his now scowling face, grunted as he gestured for us to follow.

'There's five rooms up here without heating. Let's get a move on or we'll never hear the end of it.'

'What about the room Mrs went in?' I asked.

Dawson looked shocked by the suggestion.

'Oh, good God, no. That's her ladyship's room. We'll never be allowed in there. Besides, there's no actual need, since it has an open fire.'

The grumbling groundsman took us to each room, where Holmes maintained his pretence by performing the same ritual as before, this time with more alacrity. Finally, Dawson brought us to another locked door. This, I assumed, was the room Wallace had died in. Like almost every other room on the west side of the house, it wasn't simply devoid of furniture, but of personal items and knickknacks too. With the exception of a chair and large round table, it was just another sad and unremarkable dusty room. Holmes glanced briefly around, following the pipes as he had in each previous room, stopping a few times to examine something in greater detail.

Dawson remained in the doorway. His scowl had left him. I noticed Holmes running his eyes along the wall, occasionally muttering.

'Look here,' he cried, calling our attention to the section of the wall he stood beside. 'I've found your problem. There's damage to the pipes here, you see it?'

Still reluctant to come further into the room, Dawson craned his neck to peer at what Holmes had pointed out.

'This pipe comes from the main feed. That's what makes the radiators hot up here.'

Dawson's agitation gave way to curiosity. 'Is that the reason no heat works upstairs?'

'I believe so,' Holmes said, nodding. 'There's water damage here too. Looks like something hit the pipe, there's a bloody great hole in the wall next to it.'

The groundsman grudgingly came to stand beside us. 'Water damage? Is it serious?'

'I'd say so.' Holmes ran a finger inside the broken wall. 'What made this hole?'

'Mice, probably,' Dawson offered, unconvincingly.

'Mice?' Holmes laughed. 'More like a snake, I'd say.'

'Never mind that, can you fix the pipe or not?'

'I can patch it, but it'll mean taking all this wall cladding off, and running a new pipe from the stair.' Holmes stepped back and rubbed his chin. 'Does Mrs want that done now, or shall we come back?'

'How long will it take?'

'At least three hours, maybe four.'

'That won't cut it,' Dawson said, sighing. 'I'll have to check with her, you stay here.'

'We ain't going nowhere, it's fine,' Holmes said. 'Take your time.'

When Dawson had left us, Holmes set me by the door while he made a detailed examination of the room. I noticed he took more scrapings from the floor and table. I could see a streak of wax which had spread along the table, now solidified, and formed into a pool on the floor below. Holmes filled several envelopes with it. His attention then turned to the door and the walls. The urgency of his scrutiny was far less than it was in the previous room. Holmes was now meticulously tapping along each section of wall. I took my eyes from the hallway for a moment, and when I turned back, Dawson was standing right behind me watching Holmes with a terrible expression on his face.

'Now then, you,' he said, coming to Holmes far quicker than I would have given him credit for, grabbing his arm. 'What's all this about, eh?'

To his credit, Holmes remained calm.

'Blimey, mister. I'm making sure them pipes don't go through these newer walls.'

Dawson released him. 'Oh, right? I see. Sorry.'

'You're as jumpy as a ferret,' Holmes said, patting him on the back. 'That woman of yours gives you too hard a time.'

Dawson shook his head and offered Holmes a weak smile. 'You have no idea how bad she is.'

'What did she say about the building work?' Holmes asked.

'It's no good. She won't have it. Can you make the heat bypass this room?'

'Probably not the room itself,' Holmes said, rubbing his chin.

'Couldn't you just shut the heat off to the upstairs?'

'Good idea. That's easy. We can do that.'

Holmes looked along the coiled piping, then up at me with a grin. 'What do you think, Charlie?'

'If it speeds up the work,' I said, with a genuine desire to leave. 'I'm all for it.'

Dawson, I noticed, had relaxed somewhat.

'Do that then and fix the boiler. She wants the heating on downstairs sharp. Once it's done, you can be on your way, and I can get a well-needed drink.'

Holmes left the room, and I picked up his bag of tools and followed. I heard Dawson lock the door behind us. It took Holmes a few minutes to locate the pipes on the landing. After he had shut them off, he smiled.

'There you go, that'll stop any heat going beyond this point. Let's go get that boiler up and running, shall we?'

Relieved, I followed them downstairs. Holmes worked at fixing the boiler and in hardly any time, he had it lit and working. Dawson checked a few radiators on the ground floor and returned to us happy. He then paid us and sent us away. I was more than thrilled to leave that dreary old house.

After a slow walk we reached the front lawn. From here, we joined the path that wound through giant hedges out to the lane. Holmes stopped to light a cigarette, and I glanced back at the house, my eyes drawn to movement in one of the upstairs windows. I thought, at first, it a trick of the light but as I stared up, I could just make out the silhouette of someone framed in a window, wearing what could have been a veil. I tapped Holmes on the shoulder and he turned his eyes in the direction I pointed. The figure, perhaps because we were both staring up, quickly disappeared, leaving the window empty once again.

'And now,' Holmes said, finishing and flicking his cigarette away. 'It is also time for us to depart.'

Holmes set off. I continued to stare for a moment longer, then followed him along the path, leaving Langsdale House behind.

Chapter Six

A lack of food makes you obstreperous

It seems incredible to me now, as I read through my notes, how I completely failed to spot almost all the elements Holmes determined during our investigation. Having now discovered undercover work was not really what I thought it would be, I nevertheless felt privileged to have seen my friend in action. His ability to create new personalities, whilst remaining in character and simultaneously gathering all manner of data he needed to complete his case, was remarkable. I will also admit to being grateful that for once I was not the brunt of his jokes over a foolish inability to spot him when disguised, which were irksome at the best of times.

We reached the high street, still in our characters, and we bumped into Wilkins, the young tailor's apprentice Holmes had met at the Rose and Crown, as he stepped out from his quaint shop. After a brief conversation to be polite, Holmes moved us to an estate agent's door. Holmes checked the street several times, quickly pulling out an envelope from his jacket, and pushing it through the letterbox. The sound of the town clock's bell alerted us as it struck the hour of six. I shivered at the thick grey-black cloud moving across from the horizon to meet us, as the light of the wintery day diminished. My thoughts soon turned to us heading home and the comforts it afforded. It was with a profound sense of relief that I observed Holmes hailing us a cab.

'I am eager to learn what you discovered,' I said, finally able to drop the character of Charlie and warm myself with the cab's heavy rug.

'There were some points of interest,' he said, as we cozied up for warmth.

'You obviously saw more than I did.'

'We saw the same,' Holmes reminded me. 'I have drawn several conclusions we must now test. Our work has not finished today.'

I let the inwards groan escape from my lips.

'We are to go elsewhere, at this late hour, in these ridiculous disguises?'

Holmes smiled at me. 'A touch, Watson. What has affected your mood so?'

'I am hungry, Holmes,' I replied. 'A lack of food tends to make me hungry.'

'A lack of food makes you obstreperous, Watson,' he retorted.

My mood was turning obnoxious, I admit.

'I'm tired, forgive me.'

Holmes patted my hand. 'Undercover detective work can be laborious for those who take no thrill in its art, I understand.'

His words lifted the greyness of my mind, but the pang of hunger kept me just on the edge of irritation.

'I do not blame you for wanting to expedite the day's activities, Watson. It must have been an entirely boring experience for you. I shall not require you to remain in character any further tonight, but carefully keep the attire ready in case it becomes necessary to reuse it later.'

'I will, of course.'

Holmes pulled out his clay pipe and stuffed and lit it.

'When we arrive at Baker Street, I recommend you have dinner, then take a hot bath to ease the chill from your bones. Perhaps you might visit your club as you intended to do yesterday? We still need information on Wallace, and Billings is the best person who might provide it.'

My bad temper had all but gone now. 'Consider it done. What of you? Will you be away all night?'

Holmes pulled his pipe from his mouth. 'It is unlikely you will see me before noon tomorrow.'

'Is there nothing you can tell me?' I asked, hopeful of something.

'Since you have been an enormous support, and it has caused you a degree of irritation, perhaps I will share something significant. Ask yourself one question, Watson. Where were the staff?'

I had not considered that. 'Other than the housekeeper and Dawson, we saw none.'

'Indeed. Not a single staff member. I am sure you noticed the state of the kitchen?'

'I did. I thought it odd. It looked as though it had not been cleaned in days.'

'Curious, is it not?'

'Perhaps their work is done at night?'

Holmes smiled at me. 'Put a pin in that solution, Watson. I have also been considering it, but no doubt for different reasons.'

'Meaning?'

'Meaning I have given you a clue. I hope, after your conversation with Billings, you might come back to me with an answer for it.'

The cab slowed and pulled up outside our door, and I stepped out.

'I will do my best,' I remarked, as I closed the door.

'Enjoy your evening,' came his reply.

Holmes tapped the ceiling twice, and the cab took off with him still inside.

I ascended our stair and slipped my keys into the lock. A

figure in a doorway two houses down from ours then caught my attention. There was something odd about the fellow I could not put my finger on. Perhaps it was the way he held his newspaper in that obvious way suggesting he had no intention of reading it, especially since there was hardly enough light to do so, which made me think it a ploy to conceal his identity. Whatever his motives, when the fellow noticed me looking, he turned his back and ostentatiously sashayed away.

*

My club, which is in Mayfair, was a welcoming place where I could be free of life's woes, if only for that evening. David Billings, my oldest friend and fellow doctor, had introduced me to it some years earlier. Through him, I made a small group of like-minded professional friends. My association with Sherlock Holmes had gained me, rather embarrassingly, a bit of a celebrity status amongst my colleagues and frequently, when I met up with them, the conversation would dominate with my tales of Holmes's adventures, which must have become tiresome after a while. Fortunately, I found the club empty of most of our compatriots, and so I could spend my time with Billings playing several games of billiards, which I am pleased to say ended with me as victor. When we'd put away our cues, and the staff had served brandy, we sat content to smoke a cigar in a pair of matching red-leather chairs.

'Is your old wound bothering you again?' Billings asked.

I chuckled as I relaxed. 'Noticed the limp, did you?'

'That, and the heavy eyes. You seem tired. What have you been up to?'

I made up a story about how I had overdone a long walk, or some such thing, and Billings listened with interest. I then broached the subject of Doctor Wallace with him. His eyes lit and he sat forwards.

'What's your interest?' he asked, flicking ash into the tray beside us.

'Oh, you know, just curiosity. Nothing more.'

Billings did not buy my explanation. 'Ah, so now I understand why you wanted to spend the night with me. Not for my company then, for shame?' Billings's harrumph, I could tell, was playfully meant.

'Now then,' I said, wagging a disapproving finger in his direction. 'You know well enough that I always welcome spending time with you.'

'Nice save,' he replied, chuckling. 'Holmes is taking an interest in the goings-on at Langsdale House, I take it?'

I shrugged. 'I suppose it's fair to say his interests might lie in that direction. I read something in the Times regarding the murder-suicide, and it made us both curious.'

Billings's expression suggested he accepted my explanation.

'What do you know about the Houston-Smythe family, anything?'

'Quite a bit, actually.' Billings relit his cigar and exhaled a cloud of smoke. 'Wallace had quite a reputation, in certain quarters.'

'In high-society circles, you mean?'

'You could say that. He certainly had pretty tight clients, some of them of the gentry.'

'I heard he had specific specialisations that might cause a scandal or two?'

He gave a sideways glance. 'You hear a lot for someone who claims to only have read an article in the Times. Spill the beans, Watson.'

'Well,' I said. 'Perhaps I misled you a little.'

'Ah,' Billings remarked, leaning forwards. 'I knew it. Holmes is investigating? He sent you to pump me for information, didn't he?'

'No,' I replied, a little too quickly. Billings stared at me with a half-smile. 'Well, fine, yes. But not in the way you suggest. Keep this between us, because I do not want to unintentionally compromise his investigation.'

'Mum's the word, old man. I can tell you some things, but a lot of it is just gossip.'

I pulled out my notepad. 'Do you mind if I make a few notes?'

He shook his head.

'Wallace had a half-brother high in government circles. I suppose it might have been through him he was introduced to the elite? Anyway, my understanding is, once Wallace qualified, he travelled abroad for several years, picking up along the way what can best be described as less than orthodox treatments for certain diseases. I don't know for sure where. When Wallace returned to England, he joined a practice in London, but not long after, a year maybe, he set out on his own. As you said, there's been one or two scandals with his name attached, but he avoided prosecution somehow. A few years back he took up residence at Langsdale House and set up a new practice there.'

'Most of that I knew already,' I said.

'Well, here's something you might not know. It's been suggested his wife is not a woman of any means at all. Apparently, Wallace had the money. Did you know she had the deeds for the Langsdale estate signed over to her son, and not Wallace?'

This I did not know. 'When would that have occurred?'

'On the occasion of his twenty-first birthday. Which was, I believe, a month away.'

That news held value, I felt sure.

'How did you come by this information?'

'Mostly from Pearson. He's friends with a group of solicitors. Apparently over a game of bridge, he listened to them talking about it. Pearson and Wallace were school friends. He told me Wallace had confirmed it was true.'

'That's a little unusual, isn't it?'

'I'd say. There were rumours a while back that Harold and Wallace had a poor relationship, and I wondered if that might be the reason. It turns out that might not be true. When Harold became ill, it was Wallace who cared for him, exclusively.'

I did not reveal what that illness was, as I felt it inappropriate.

Billings leant towards me. 'Maybe that's why he killed Harold? To stop the estate going to him? Doesn't explain why he'd kill himself though. Remorse maybe?'

I shrugged. Wallace's death was still a mystery. It was almost certain he did not kill himself, but I did not feel it fitting to divulge those facts.

'How was Harold's relationship with his mother?'

'That I can't be sure of,' Billings replied. 'When Harold's ownership of the house came into force, it would mean transferring the property rights over to him. I don't suppose she'd want to cause him any upset, in case he put her out?'

'Do you think she was in any danger of that?'

He sat back in his chair. 'Maybe. No one really knows what happens in private. She might have been an awful woman. Not much is really said about her, except in connection with Wallace. They had a first-rate bond, as far as I heard. I can't give you a suitable answer there.'

I thought for a moment. 'Have you ever had occasion to visit Langsdale yourself?'

My friend gave me a shocked look, then vigorously shook his head. 'The very idea! It's not somewhere I would ever go.' He narrowed his eyes a little. 'Is that why Holmes asked you to talk with me? Does he suspect I'm a client?'

His suspiciousness caught me off guard. It really was quite uncharacteristic.

'Holmes doesn't always confide his thoughts to me. It seems unlikely that was his intention… but what do you mean, a client? Of Wallace?'

My friend raised an eyebrow. 'Have you not been there yourself?'

I confessed my day's activities, which Billings listened to without comment.

'It is a very a strange and dreary house,' I concluded. 'It's empty of staff and furniture. It apparently once had staff, but they were moved to an outer house on the property a few months back. We didn't get to visit it, but I imagine one is coming since I know how thorough Holmes can be.'

'I shouldn't imagine even Holmes would be that cruel to you,' he remarked.

'Why would you say that?'

Billings looked at me with something akin to surprise and disbelief on his face. 'You don't know what really goes on up there, do you?'

'Clearly,' I replied, my irritation now flaring. 'Since you and Holmes have all the answers, perhaps you would be kind enough to furnish me with some?'

Billings put a hand on my knee. 'My dear friend, I didn't mean to offend. I simple assumed you would know.'

'Know what?'

'It's only the worst-kept secret in town. Langsdale House is a brothel.'

Billings had opened my eyes to a truth clear from the outset. I inwardly chastised my foolishness. Sergeant Birch alluded to it, which I had missed, and of course I could not forget young Popplewick's plea for help. Had Holmes known all along? It seemed he may have. I recalled his suggestion Elsie was probably a prostitute. Holmes warned me against delving too deeply into her disappearance, refusing to take Popplewick's case on. Holmes's warnings now appeared justifiably warranted. It was not for the first time I felt shame in my inability to see the obvious. My friend read some of this as he ordered us another brandy. Billings, being a younger man, appeared to accept the vileness of the seedier aspects of our society with far greater ease than I.

The brandy calmed me, if only a little. 'How has this place been able to evade the law?'

He shrugged. 'Money and powerful people, I suspect. How else?'

How else indeed?

*

My thoughts dwelled on the improprieties of Langsdale House as my cab took me back to Baker Street. It was a little after ten when I ascended to our rooms, grateful to find Mrs Hudson had maintained our sitting-room fire until she herself had retired. Although dying, it was still hot enough to catch. I stared into those roaring flames, attempting to put aside my disgust at the entire affair.

In my solitude, I attempted to put the facts I had learnt from Billings to good use. I considered all I had discovered. If the case had involved Mrs Houston-Smythe in some form other than as a witness, a potential answer might be that she murdered Wallace in retribution for him killing Harold. Perhaps she had put the gun in his right hand by mistake. It certainly worked with the evidence of the jam on his left hand and cuff, implying his left-handedness. Billings said mother and son had a good relationship, supported by her signing the estate over to him. She certainly would not be the first mother to commit a murder to avenge a dead child. Was Mrs Houston-Smythe aware of the sordid nature of what went on at her property? Maybe she was the controlling influence? Or perhaps, like me, just innocently ignorant? This felt more agreeable.

Was Wallace the man in the shadows? I knew he'd spent time abroad learning medical techniques which weren't considered, as Billings put it, orthodox. Yet somehow this felt wrong. It is true I disagreed with Wallace's choice in employing alternatives to commonly prescribed treatments, but that did not make him an evil man. There was no evidence yet that proved that Wallace had murdered Harold. Given that it appeared they enjoyed a friendship, I could not imagine what circumstances might lead him to want to kill the boy, unless perhaps he did so because his condition had become too advanced? A mercy killing, perhaps? Somehow this felt wrong. As a doctor, Wallace would have done everything he could to control Harold's condition, even if he could not eradicate it entirely. There was also the implied avoidance of his alleged criminal liabilities to be considered. Was blackmail a consideration? I suppose if Harold was blackmailing Wallace over some liable situation, then it is conceivable, however unlikely, that he killed him to put an end to it.

What of Harold Houston? A boy of twenty with hardly any life experience, yet a clear and demonstratable familiarity with unhealthy sexual practices. Was he just a victim? Or was he running the brothel? Could Harold have contracted syphilis at the house? It was certainly the right environment for it. But Harold's condition was in an advanced stage, and he could not have been in any mind to do anything other than pin all hope in his mercuric treatment. The condition of his body suggested he may not have survived much beyond a month or two.

My thoughts then turned to Chief Inspector Mulgrave. What part did he play in the Langsdale House affair? What was his reason for closing the investigation down? Protecting members of the gentry, or an even higher dignitary? That made sense, but then it might be something less conspiratorial than that. Was Mulgrave simply another client?

My list of questions generated more. I had little hope of realising any uncomplicated solutions to answer any of them. I decided it was best to put them out of my mind. Holmes would have the answers I sought. It would be impossible to persuade him to divulge anything, until he was ready to do so, and so I resigned myself to wait for his explanations.

Chapter Seven

I owe you an apology, in that regard

By mid-afternoon that following day, I had not seen or heard anything from Holmes. Since the weather had warmed a little, my thoughts centred on the idea of a walk. As I made plans, Mrs Hudson came in with a telegram and interrupted them.

'It's from Mr Holmes,' she said, handing it to me.

The telegram commanded me to come to an address in Notting Hill in the guise of my alter ego, Charlie. An hour later, following the instructions Holmes laid out, I exited my cab at Westbourne Park and followed Ladbroke Grove to a newsagent. There, I purchased the specified paper and sat at the bench. It was not long before Holmes joined me, still in the same disguise from the day before.

'Follow me,' he whispered.

We wove a strange path in silence up to Ladbroke Grove Station, where Holmes purchased two smoker tickets and ushered me into a waiting train. He hardly said a word, electing only to smoke his clay pipe and throw furtive glances here and there at the other passengers on board. Five stops later, we exited the train at Hammersmith. Holmes weaved along alleyways ending at a café where he finally relaxed.

'Forgive my precautions,' he said, sipping at the hot tea he'd ordered. 'It has been a harrowing night, but we are safe from any prying eyes and unwanted ears.'

'I noticed a fellow last night at Baker Street. Is this who you are attempting to avoid?'

'No, not that particular fellow, but I am being careful. These people have no interest in you, fortunately.'

'I don't suppose whoever it was recognised me in this disguise,' I remarked.

Holmes leant forward. 'We are dealing with a hard group, Watson. These are not commonplace criminals. I thought about changing my appearance, but I realised I would gain no information by doing so.'

I noticed how tired Holmes looked.

'Have you been up all night?'

'As I said, it has been harrowing.' He rubbed at his neck. I noticed a mottled bruise on it.

'You're injured,' I said. 'Let me look.'

With a quick shake of his head, he forbade it. I understood why. My doctorly instincts would undo the caution he'd displayed, and those instincts, I knew, would put us in further danger, so I sat back down.

'I injured my pride only, dear Watson, but enough of that. Tell me about your visit with Billings.'

I gave a brief recount of our conversation, including as much detail as I could. When I fell silent, Holmes sat lost in thought for several minutes.

'You've done well,' he said.

'There was value in what he said, then?'

'Yes,' he replied, attacking a bowl of beef stew that had just arrived. 'The facts regarding Wallace and Harold's relationship with Mrs Houston-Smythe, along with the change of ownership of Langsdale House need corroborating.'

'Might we consider blackmail?'

Holmes frowned. 'What put that idea into your brain?'

'Well,' I said. 'It strikes me we do have evidence to consider it.'

'Such as?'

'The liable cases.'

'What cases? Wallace had no charges brought against him,' Holmes remarked.

'I know. But suppose, for a moment, Harold had something on Wallace. Might it be enough for him to silence the boy?'

Holmes paused for a moment. 'Interesting. Go on.'

'We know Wallace didn't kill himself. What if he killed Harold and went upstairs to quieten his nerve, where his wife followed and killed him in retaliation? It fits the facts.'

'It fits some facts. What about the jam?'

'We know the answer to that. To cover the mercuric treatments.'

'Why did Wallace not leave the spoon with the jar of jam? Why take it with him?'

That was a good question. One I had given little thought to.

'I suspect the jam idea was spur of the moment,' I suggested. 'Wallace's state of mind must have been affected badly by his act of murder. He probably forgot he was holding it.'

Holmes shook his head. 'That won't do, Watson. The jam points to a person in control of their senses.'

'I don't see how you can say that?'

'Did the jam arrive before or after Harold died?'

'After, surely?'

Holmes inclined his head. 'You propose Wallace killed Harold then went to the pantry for a jar of jam? Even if the timeline allowed for this, which it does not, that act surely indicates a sound state of mind?'

'Before then,' I offered.

Holmes shook his head. 'But that implies Harold's murder was premeditated, which does not fit your state-of-mind theory either.'

I sighed. 'Well, you have an answer for everything.'

'Possibly,' he said, chuckling. 'I am gratified you are applying yourself. Wallace took that spoon for a reason.'

'For what purpose?'

'I cannot say.' Holmes was thoughtful for a moment. 'Did Billings explain what the Langsdale estate represents?'

'Yes. He said it's a brothel.'

Holmes nodded. 'It is becoming a sordid little adventure.'

After several minutes he had finished his stew, mopping the remains with a crust of bread, and pushing his bowl aside.

'Forgive me. I have not eaten since yesterday lunch time.'

'What of your investigation?' I asked. 'Have you gained any new insights?'

'My night was not without its moments of interest. These are deep waters, Watson, as you have perhaps determined from my precautions? We cannot be complacent, nor ignore the elements of danger this case has manifested.'

'The results of which led to that bruising?'

Holmes lit his pipe and smoked for a moment. 'Yes,' he said. 'But that is a discussion for another time.'

I also took up my pipe while Holmes detailed his night's activities.

'First, there are several events running in parallel. I have narrowed my focus to three elements I consider have connection to one another. The death of Harold and Wallace Houston-Smythe, the brothel running on the estate and,' he paused and smiled, 'the disappearance of young Mr Popplewick's love interest, Elsie.'

I raised an eyebrow. 'Then you do consider his case important?'

'I owe you an apology, in that regard. I have been less than candid. I conceived that the disappearance of Elsie might be important and now have evidence which corroborates it.'

I was happy Holmes considered Popplewick's case, if perhaps a little irked at his methods of putting me off.

'You are right to be annoyed, but it was essential you did not communicate with this young man, as I knew you would, had I acquiesced to your suggestion of taking on his case.'

'You could have just told me that,' I said.

'I could have, but lacked the data to warrant doing so.'

'And you have it now?'

'Somewhat. The puzzle is incomplete, but there is at least a picture forming.'

I sipped my tea. Despite my annoyance, it did not entirely surprise me. Holmes was, at least, consistent in that regard. It was not the first time his unemotional brain caused me frustration, and I suspected it would not be the last. I let that annoyance go.

'Finding Elsie will bring comfort to Mr Popplewick,' I said. 'The boy is taken by her, despite her profession.'

'And yet,' Holmes said with a sad look, 'it will only bring him anguish, as I alluded to when you broached the topic.'

'Why do you say that?'

'Popplewick answered it himself. Did he not suggest something terrible had occurred?'

'True,' I said, remembering the boy's emotional plea. 'He seemed certain of it.'

'His instincts were not wrong.'

My heart sunk. 'You seem certain, why?'

'Because, dear Watson. We may have already witnessed what became of this unfortunate woman.'

'Witnessed? Where?'

'At the morgue. Surely you recall the body of the burnt woman?'

'Good God.'

Holmes, who had seen my expression drop at that disclosure, reached out and patted my hand.

'Quite so. Now, perhaps, you will forgive my methods of dissuading your involvement?'

'Of course. Was she murdered?'

'Almost certainly. I am sorry.'

The sadness and guilt I felt over the unfortunate woman's demise, along with the idea I might have to explain it to Mr Popplewick, threatened to overwhelm me. I kept silent for several minutes. As a doctor, I had occasionally been the bearer of terrible news, but somehow this felt entirely different. However, I could not allow myself to dwell. I shook off my reverie and expunged those thoughts proper.

'How do we unravel all these threads? What does it all mean?' I asked.

'We can start by recognising that the first event which precipitated everything from that point forwards, might not be as it seems.'

'You mean the murder of Harold?'

Holmes shook his head. 'That was not the first event.'

My brain ran over the information I could recall. 'Three months back, then? When the servants moved out?'

'Not quite.' He smiled encouragingly. 'Although I must congratulate you on your thinking.'

Holmes waited for an answer, and for the life of me I could not see what he was looking for. I racked my brain, running over Billings's and Birch's conversations. Had they said it and I not paid attention? There was only one thing I could recall.

'The purchase of Langsdale House?'

Holmes sighed. 'I suppose it was too much to hope you might see it.'

'Well tell me then,' I growled, crossing my arms. 'Your ingenuity can then amaze me.'

Holmes raised an eyebrow. 'Perhaps I will keep you in suspense as punishment for your lack of imagination, and your easy arousal.'

Sherlock Holmes, at the best of times, could be entirely impossible.

'I misdirected my frustration, Holmes, and I apologise.'

Holmes inclined his head. 'Accepted. Let me ask a question. Who exactly is Mrs Harriot Dawson?'

I frowned, since we both knew the answer to that, I thought the question was odd.

'The horribly austere housekeeper you fell into at the house?'

'Exactly. But who is she, Watson? That is the question

which beats at my brain.'

I thought I saw what he was getting at. 'Yes, we have little information on her. Didn't Birch say she came from some position in Ireland?'

'There is the nucleus for all of my questions, I fancy. Do you not consider it curious that the Houston-Smythe and Dawson families all came from foreign parts?'

I hadn't considered that. 'It is a little coincidental,' I offered.

'Coincidence, in my profession, is far rarer than you would think. I consider coincidences facts: lone facts with no immediate correlation to any others. Given what we know, in this case, the odds are enormously against it being a coincidence.'

'I'm not sure I follow. The previous owners, Hodgkin something-or-other, both travelled extensively in the Americas if I recall correctly. Surely, there is your link?'

Holmes sat up in his chair. 'I could not gain much in the way of useful information on that score. Both died, as we were told, in an accident abroad. There is a family in America, of course, but finding them may present further challenges.'

'Do you think those deaths were not the result of an accident?'

Holmes shook his head. 'There is little evidence to make a reasonable supposition. Certainly nothing in England that might help us. But we cannot get past the fact that their deaths were officially registered in America as accidental.'

This surprised me. 'There was an inquest, correct? Can't we get the files from a clerk at the coroner's court?'

Holmes sighed. 'Inquests dealing with cases of accidental death in foreign parts are hardly ever given serious consideration, especially when there are no family members or witnesses present to question. I was able to take a peek at that file and it had some points of interest, but it is thin. Judges routinely preside and give verdict over cases with little or no substantive evidence. This was an open and shut case. The documents presented, though weak in substance, came from the official police. Cecil and Clara Hodgkin-Tramwell died while boating off the coast of New Jersey. They were staying at the Hotel Albion. They booked a ferry which collided with another and sank. The verdict by the New Jersey coroner was accidental drowning due to a maritime collision. The New Jersey police sent those details to Scotland Yard.'

'It all seems rather conclusive, then.'

'And yet something about the evidence file irked me. I wonder if you can deduce who supplied the information to the inquest?'

'Mulgrave?'

Holmes beamed. 'Yes, our less-than-friendly Chief Inspector Mulgrave. We cannot assume anything untoward, since the evidence came directly from the New Jersey police, but it appears to be another of those obtuse little coincidences.'

'We do seem inundated with them,' I admitted.

'Meaning they are nothing of the sort. This housekeeper who... how did Bradstreet put it? Seemed below her station? Now that we have observed her, I believe I understand why he thought that. Mrs Dawson arrives from Ireland with her ineffectual drunkard husband, whom she clearly despises. They have no traceable backgrounds. None. As far as I can ascertain, they do not exist.'

'You believe the Dawsons coming to Langsdale House is the first event?'

Holmes smiled. 'Precisely so.'

'Are you saying that we must investigate the Dawsons, before we address Bradstreet's concerns?'

Holmes finished his tea. 'No. For now, we stick to Harold and Wallace. I know how Harold died and have strong suspicions on who murdered Wallace. The problem is, I can prove none of it.'

'You'll get to the truth, Holmes. I have faith.'

'Bless you,' he said. 'Your faith is of inestimable comfort.'

'You positively concluded Wallace was left-handed, no doubt, from those scraps of paper found in the rubbish at the house?'

Holmes pulled several crumpled sheets of paper from his pocket.

'Yes. It was a simple matter to find these samples of his writing. The penmanship of a left-handed man is quite unmistakable.'

'You also took scrapings and several other things from the floors of both rooms, as I recall. Will that evidence not help?'

Holmes sighed. 'Not on their own. A fibre here, a drop of wax there, each helpful when forming a theory, but entirely useless without any connecting data.'

'We're no further forward, then?'

'Hardly that,' he said, cleaning his pipe into the ashtray. 'As with all our cases, we must work each thread till we exhaust it. I have several others yet to pull on.'

'What shall we do next?'

Holmes's features hardened. 'The first thing we must do is get this band of dogs off our tails. For that, I will need to cash in a favour.'

'From your underground contacts?'

Holmes nodded and his expression became harder. 'These fellows are usually linked, in some fashion. I know a few players.'

'Honour amongst thieves, is that it?'

'Something like that,' Holmes remarked, placing his pipe in his pocket.

'What of Harmony?' I asked.

'She is doing her part.'

'But is Harmony, as Elsie clearly was, in mortal danger?'

Holmes shook his head. 'There is danger, Watson, but for the moment Harmony is safe. How long that remains, I cannot say for certain.'

'Then we must act at once,' I said. 'These people are murderers, Holmes. If they killed Elsie, then they would think nothing of killing Harmony too. I do not want to find myself looking at another burnt corpse, thinking we could have avoided or prevented it somehow.'

'And yet,' Holmes cautioned me, 'to extricate her now

would almost certainly compromise her position and that really would be her end.' He put up a hand to quash my retort. 'As much as it continues to irk you, we must be patient and trust in her abilities which, as I have continually assured you, are considerable.'

I still did not like it, but let the topic drop.

'Now that we have eaten, I will head out and see to these dogs trailing us. I will also attempt to move Harmony to a safer environment. There are some tasks I need your assistance with, Watson. You might want to take some notes.'

Chapter Eight

Our case moves forward, thanks to your efforts

'You understand your assignment?' Holmes asked, as we walked away from the café.

'It's clear. Should I not return to Baker Street first? I hardly think I can elicit the information you requested dressed as I currently am.'

Holmes shook his head. 'You will be surprised at what a shabby suit will get you. Do not be put off should your inquiries amount to nothing. It is a long shot. Say little. Remain as though you were given this task from a master, that way you will not give yourself away by your obvious intellect. I will meet you at Baker Street this evening.' With nothing more left to say, he left me with my list of errands.

Holmes had asked me to visit shops that sold candles from Hammersmith to South Kensington. I was looking for a particular brand of dark-green candle. I was to hand each shopkeeper the note Holmes had written, and retain it for the next, once I had the specific candle he required. Under no circumstances was I to engage in any conversation, especially should I be asked why I was seeking them. Should such a conversation occur, then I would feign ignorance, which required no skill since Holmes had not explained why I was making those enquires. When I discovered the brand he requested, I was to purchase one only. The walk from Hammersmith was pleasant. It was not an arduous job by any means.

As it turned out, the particular style and brand of candle was not that popular. On my journey, I came upon six shops in Hammersmith that sold candles, but of those I entered, only five had what I was looking for, and only three were willing to let me make a single purchase. That seemed significant, so I made a note of those too. Most of the shops I visited were used to a certain class of customer and spared no time in completing a transaction – perhaps because they wished for me to leave and not upset their usual clientele. It appeared Holmes had been correct about my appearance and I vacated their premises with hardly any conversation at all. After one or two additional shop visits along my route to South Kensington, I completed that task. With five candles in my bag, I moved on to the next.

One task he set, which caused me the least concern, was to visit with two chemists. I decided on a different approach to the one Holmes directed, as I felt sure mine would garner better results. It worked, and I found it easy to get the answers I needed.

My last assignment had me visit a local domestic hiring agency. The light of the day was waning when I made my call to a young lady named Sally Porter, who happily answered my questions. With my information on the number of staff Sally had supplied Langsdale House, amongst others, completed, I closed my book and headed home.

*

It was at around seven, roughly two hours after my return, when Holmes entered our sitting room. Although his exhaustion was clear, he wasted no time in removing his disguise. When he returned to our table, he was dressed in his usual clothes and mouse-coloured dressing gown.

'How did you do?' he asked. I opened my bag and he peered in. 'Oh, you did very well indeed. Splendid, Watson. I cannot thank you enough.'

Holmes pulled out candles and lined them up together. Aside from imperfections in their moulds, they were almost identical.

'To the naked eye they may appear so,' Holmes remarked, depositing each onto his chemical table. 'Let us see if the microscope agrees with you.'

'Mrs Hudson said she would serve our dinner as soon as we called her. Shall I have her wait?'

Holmes smiled at me. 'Dinner! Quite so. Let us eat and you can tell me about the other tasks I set you.'

Mrs Hudson served a fabulous roasted leg of lamb, with all the trimmings, and we were soon engaged in that mixed bag of eating and talking.

'The two chemists I spoke with gave little in the way of direct answers. They both said that Mrs Dawson regularly collected the prescriptions Wallace wrote. I could not get any information on what those prescriptions contained, at least...'

'I feared as much. It was a long shot,' Holmes said, interrupting me.

'At least,' I said again, slower, to make my point. 'Not initially.'

Holmes raised an eyebrow. I think I might cherish his surprised look for some time.

'You mean you discovered what those prescriptions contained?'

'I did. Both chemists supplied blue mass calomel for Mrs Houston-Smythe. It is fairly common and has a wide application from toothache to childbirth, but because of its mercuric chloride content—'

'It can treat syphilis?' Holmes interjected.

'Yes. Blue mass is a little unusual because there cannot be

any definitive dosing. Blue pill would have been a far better choice. Bradford and Company on the South Kensington high street were, at least until as recently as two weeks ago, filling a chloral hydrate prescription for Mrs Houston-Smythe as well. The last order occurred just days before Wallace's death. The last filling of calomel occurred a week previous to that.'

Holmes clapped his hands. 'Bravo, my dear friend. I admit I suspected this avenue to produce limited results, but you have exceeded expectations. How were you able to get such a detailed account?'

I beamed. 'By applying your methods.'

We had by now finished the last of our meal.

'Coercion will not work on reputable chemists, the law on their practices is specific to official... of course,' he said, pointing at me. 'I am a fool. A doctor would have the legal access necessary to review a prescription register.'

I laughed. 'You have it. I know you set me with a specific agenda, but I made an appeal to both chemists, explaining an anomaly over a prescription I had issued. They are legally obliged to assist, if they had filled it. Both chemists were helpful, but as you know, it is their practice to keep a review of the register supervised. Luckily, at both times, a customer distracted the chemist and left me alone with it.'

'Again, I congratulate you. Good luck favoured you indeed, since you could not know a customer, in both instances, would give you the opportunity to make that study.'

'Could I not?' I said, raising my eyebrow.

'Watson, you devil! Do I deduce from your smugness that you coerced someone to distract them?'

'As I said. I followed your methods. It cost me a few shillings, but the results were worth it.'

Holmes laughed. 'You really did do it very well. I assume you made a note of all the details?'

I handed him my notebook. 'I have also jotted answers to your other questions, specifically the movement of staff at Langsdale. There have been several appointments over the past six months. Apparently, Sally only supplied girls with certain attributes. Their experience did not seem to factor. The requirements were stringent, but she didn't consider them usual. I suppose we know the answer to that?'

Holmes read through my notes, nodding. 'Yes, but the data is telling and may not relate to the idea of a brothel.'

Holmes continued to read for several minutes, while I drank the rest of my wine. Eventually, he handed the notes back to me.

'Most of this I already knew. I can now, at least, attribute it to a specific source which will be necessary in the event of a trial.'

We took coffee in the chairs beside the fire. Holmes lit his long-stemmed pipe.

'Our case moves forward, thanks to your efforts.'

The praise and Mrs Hudson's meal had done much to raise my spirits. I relaxed, filling my pipe, looking to Holmes now for answers of his day.

'What can you tell me of your exploits?'

Holmes however seemed not to hear me. As he smoked, I watched him unconsciously pull the pipe from his mouth and rub its amber tip along his bottom lip. He then took a long pull, exhaling the smoke over his head, and repeated this cycle several times. I finished my coffee, pleased to note that Holmes's dreamy, faraway expression had lifted. When his eyes focused on me, he smiled.

'Oh, my dear fellow,' he said. 'We have a long and dangerous day of work ahead of us. I will give you an explanation, of course, but in an hour. For now, I must think. I beg you not to speak until that hour has elapsed.'

While Holmes sat smoking, I read through my notes. Careful not to disturb him, I began adding more substance, so as not to lose any threads we were currently working on. At some point I dozed off, only to be startled awake by an exclamation from Holmes. I turned in my chair to see him sat at his chemical station.

Holmes looked. 'Did I wake you?'

I checked the clock. It was almost eleven. Some two hours had since passed. I came alongside him and he stood, indicating to his microscope, where I replaced him at the lens.

'What am I looking at?'

'A sample of paraffin wax, distilled from coal and oil shales.'

I looked up at him and frowned. 'Candle wax?'

'Precisely. I have made a study of candles over the years. I had a case, before your time, for George Wilson. Now there is an interesting subject. A religious man born of English and Scottish parentage. His father, William, was co-founder of Price's Candles.'

'Aren't they one of the largest manufacturers of candles in England?'

'The world, Watson. George is a fine chemist. Price's pioneering of implementing the technique of steam distillation enabled them to manufacture candles from a wide variety of raw organic materials. This imagination put them far above their competition. The company has had to make new strides because of more recent technological innovations. Now that Edison's incandescent light bulb is becoming popular, candles may soon be a thing of the past. Still, they have taken advantage of that decline by moving into more lucrative business ventures, such as lubricants.'

'Do you really think Edison's inventions will completely replace the candle?' I asked. The idea seemed fanciful.

'Well,' Holmes said, shrugging. 'Perhaps not entirely. I suspect their transition to a more decorative application will shortly follow.'

Holmes replaced me in the chair and looked into the lens. 'Men like Edison are modernising our world at a rate that defies belief. However, let us return to the present, and our paraffin wax. While you were sleeping, I made a scraping from each of the candles you purchased and compared it to a sample I collected from Langsdale House. Under the lens, I could find a positive match.'

'That's wonderful.'

Holmes took the candle over to the dining room table. 'It was an exact a match as I could hope for, to the one used at the house. Specifically, the one that fell when Wallace's body hit the table.'

'What was the purpose of matching it?'

'For my experiment. Now, kindly pick up this newspaper and follow me down to the street.'

Holmes took the lit candle, and we descended to the pavement outside. Under the glow of the gas lamps, I watched Holmes draw a line with chalk, then followed him as he set off on a measured walk away from our door, stopping as he put up a hand. Holmes then bent down and made another line with the chalk.

'That is two hundred steps. We can now begin my experiment. Place a sheet of newspaper down at this end, then one at the other. Wait there for me. When I give you a signal, I want you to time my progress, stopping when I reach and touch you. Understood?'

'Perfectly,' I replied and did as he asked.

Holmes put his candle on the street and several minutes later, he gave me the signal. When Holmes reached and touched me, I gave him a time of three minutes and fifteen seconds.

Holmes picked up the newspaper and studied it under the gas lamp. He then folded it carefully and put it into his left pocket. I replaced it with a fresh sheet. He took another and moved to his starting position. Holmes's second progress took longer than his previous attempt. When he reached me, I noted a time of five minutes and twenty-five seconds. Holmes went through the same ritual with the paper and put it into his right pocket. He then collected his candle and we both went back inside.

As we warmed ourselves with brandy by the fire, Holmes filled his pipe and lit it.

'Did you get the results you hoped?'

Holmes nodded. 'I can be reasonably sure, now, who murdered both Wallace and Harold, and can also confirm the order in which they both died.'

'Well,' I said. 'Don't hold back.'

'But, sadly, I must, dear Watson. I must test other assessments first. We are a stage further, that is all. The how, in this case, is answered. Now I we must determine the why.'

'Can you at least tell me these devils spying on us are no longer a concern?'

Holmes put a hand on my shoulder. 'I can confirm we shall have no further interference on that front. To forestall your next question, I have men I trust looking out for Harmony. They will let no harm come to her.'

'That is a relief,' I said. 'May I ask a question?'

He gestured for me to do so.

'Who do you think is running this brothel?'

'You lead me into the dangerous territory of supposition. I cannot know for sure, but one thing I do know is that the knowledge holds little value for now.'

'What do you mean? Has something happened?'

'Let me just say its activities are no longer of serious concern to us and leave it there.'

This news startled me. 'I am very pleased to hear it, if a little confused.'

'We may yet have cause to concern ourselves with it later, but for the moment the business falls firmly into Inspector Bradstreet's arena. And there I would like it to remain.'

'You've seen Bradstreet then?'

Holmes nodded. 'As have you.'

I frowned. 'I don't recall…'

'Who do you think you spotted lurking in the doorway the other night?'

'That was Bradstreet? But why?'

'On my instructions. I could think of no one better than Bradstreet and his men, as I needed Baker Street monitored with good cause.'

'What cause?'

Holmes's expression turned grave. 'I had reasons to fear for yours and Mrs Hudson's safety.'

I felt annoyed and expressed my disappointment. 'You could not trust me with these concerns? I am a soldier, Holmes. I should think I could do a better job monitoring the house, since I spotted him almost immediately.'

'My dear Watson, not the house, the street. Let me be clear. I know you can take care of yourself, and if my precautions have annoyed you, I apologise. You spotted Bradstreet because I told him to make himself obvious when you arrived. With the idea of someone lurking in the street, I imagine you took extra precautions when you locked the doors and windows, correct?'

'That's true,' I replied, my annoyance lessoning.

'Exactly. With those precautions taken, Mrs Hudson, I knew, would be protected since you most probably slept lightly with your old service revolver under your pillow.'

'I did indeed.' I chuckled. His levity caused my annoyance to wane completely.

'There, now. I considered your reactions. After that, I had little reason to feel concern for either yours or Mrs Hudson's safety. You noticed there was no one then today? I know my Watson. At the first sign of trouble the military man in you would make yourself ready.'

Holmes had a way of helping you up and dusting you off, just after he'd knocked you down. I turned my thoughts back to Langsdale House.

'This entire business gets more and more convoluted by the second,' I said, sighing.

Holmes put his pipe into the ashtray. 'The answers will not be long in coming. Now,' he said, yawning. 'I am overcome by the efforts of the past two days. If you would excuse me, I think it is time I head to my bedroom for some well earnt sleep. I therefore bid you good night.'

Holmes finished his brandy and slipped away, leaving me wide awake and with even more questions than I had the evening before.

Chapter Nine

We might both come to regret that you didn't

It was nearly nine o'clock when I made my way down to the sitting room. Holmes was up reading a paper when I joined him for breakfast. I had slept poorly, and the evidence of it must have been clear to Holmes, because he quietly poured coffee and handed me a cup. After taking a few sips, I gratefully felt an instant rejuvenation. I attacked a plate of bacon and eggs, and soon after pushed the plate away in satisfaction.

'Are you recovered enough from your restless night to discuss our activities of the day?' Holmes asked.

We moved to the fire, and I filled and lit my morning pipe.

'What had you in mind?'

'We will start by focusing on Sergeant Birch's recommendation to visit the records office at Scotland Yard. Then we will follow up my enquiries at the American Embassy. This will take us to lunch, where I have arranged for Bradstreet and Mulgrave to join us, at the Diogenes Club.'

'Will we need our disguises again?'

'No, those disguises are of no further practical use anymore.'

'Will Mycroft be joining us?'

Holmes shook his head. 'Mycroft and I are of the opinion he should not appear. We might put him in a delicate position by any well-intentioned interference.'

'More and more mysterious,' I said, chuckling.

'Quite.' Holmes put down his pipe. 'Let us be ready to leave in twenty minutes. A cab will arrive in thirty.'

The clock struck ten-thirty as Mrs Hudson informed us that our cab was waiting. Not long after we were on our way to Scotland Yard. Holmes instructed the cab driver to wait, and we went inside.

The duty sergeant took us into the records office and after a brief discussion with Holmes, he left us to our research. Holmes began by pulling giant black leather-bound volumes from the shelves, flicking through several pages from those of interest. Holmes quickly built a collection of discarded volumes. I did not know what he was looking for so I elected to make myself useful, and put back any he dispensed with. Holmes scrutinized unsolved case records.

A triumphant grunt from Holmes pierced the quiet, and I turned to see a look of delight on my friend's face. His eyes shone like beacons and I knew he'd discovered something significant. He slapped a finger on the page. 'Got you! Well done, Sergeant Birch.'

'You found something of interest?' I said, coming beside him.

'Precisely what Birch wanted us to find.' He turned the record book towards me. 'See for yourself.'

I read the title of the page he had selected. It read: *Murder-Suicide, Langsdale House.* Dated 1849.

'Forty years previous,' Holmes said, rubbing his hands together. 'Now we are getting somewhere. Look at the notes.'

'How extraordinary,' I said, as I began reading.

'The extraordinary, the grotesque, the inexplicable. That is what I live for, Watson. It has often been my observation that people of average intelligence, who find themselves in difficult situations, almost always seek a path of least resistance when attempting to discover solutions to their problems. These actions yield some results, but not always those desired. I suppose it is only natural for people of common intellect. But to those who train themselves to think logically and rise above mediocrity, they will almost always find a solution where people of average intelligence could never hope to do.'

'You are, of course, describing yourself.' I said with a smirk.

Holmes took my humour with good grace. 'Were the context different, I admit, I might make a similar narrative in the way you suggest. But,' he said, coming beside me to examine the record. 'I refer entirely to a particular class of criminal, although the usage of the word "criminal" in this context seems unkind. These people sit above a common thief or murderer, Watson. They are intellectuals. Couple this brainpower with iniquitous tendencies and what is the result? An adversary who, under normal circumstances, should never have a reason to fear being caught.'

'Until Sherlock Holmes is on the case, eh?'

Holmes smiled. 'Quite so.'

'But this is incredible, Holmes,' I remarked as I read on. 'This record details the murder of Patricia Hodgkin-Tramwell, and the suicide of her husband, Colonel James Hodgkin-Tramwell. Presumably the parents of the now deceased Cecil Hodgkin-Tramwell?'

'Exactly. What are the odds of a second murder-suicide occurring in the same house?'

'Low, I should imagine.'

'Would you kindly summarise the notes for me?'

'The records state the attending officer declared Colonel Hodgkin-Tramwell to have murdered his Patricia and then killed himself.'

'Sound familiar?'

'Too familiar.' I read on. 'Now this *is* interesting. The domestics, along with their children, were questioned, and each gave a varying account of what had actually happened. It seems the testimonies agreed the couple were unhappy and often engaged in violent quarrels. On the night in question, some reports suggest they engaged in a ferocious argument, which culminated in their deaths. But not all the witnesses agreed to that. It goes on to say they found no weapon with the colonel or his wife. Despite an extensive investigation the motive for Colonel Hodgkin-Tramwell's actions was never properly realised, and no one admitted to having removed the weapon.' I looked up at Holmes. 'This is extraordinary, Holmes. How could anyone conclude it was murder-suicide without finding a weapon?'

'It was a different time. Investigations were almost always concentrated on witness accounts. The case was most probably concluded on the balance of those testimonies.'

I scanned further into the notes. 'The coroner concluded a member of household staff probably took the weapon, out of some misguided loyalty to their master.'

'Not an unreasonable supposition.'

'The coroner listed Patricia's death as murder at the hand of the colonel, but the colonel's death was listed as suicide.'

'There could be a case for both having been murdered, but without further evidence, there is little chance of conclusively proving what happened.'

Holmes pulled out his notebook and scribbled several notes.

'It is a pretty little problem, eh, friend Watson? Two cases in similar circumstances, both occurring in the same house forty years apart.'

'It is a shame you were not available to assist the police back then.' I chuckled.

Holmes turned to me and I noticed the brilliance of his eyes as they twinkled in the reflected soft light of the room. 'The case does remain unsolved.'

I laughed. 'You cannot possibly mean to say you can solve this, and a forty-year-old case as well?'

Holmes said nothing as he picked up the record and read. When he had absorbed all he could, he closed and handed it back to me.

'Thanks to Sergeant Birch we have what we needed. Our next visit will be to the American Embassy, and then lunch.'

The journey from Victoria Embankment to Westminster was a short one. Our cab pulled up outside the United States Embassy in Victoria Road, and Holmes instructed me to wait. The day had turned warmer, so I remained outside, and smoked. When Holmes returned, he instructed the driver to take us to the Diogenes Club for our luncheon appointment.

'Were your enquiries successful?' I asked.

Holmes looked up from the pages of a file he'd returned with and closed it with a smile.

'Somewhat. This file contains a copy of the New Jersey coroner's report on the Hodgkin-Tramwell deaths. It corroborates the facts as we knew them. The detail requires scrutiny, but there is no time for that now because we are nearing our final destination.'

The cab pulled up outside the Diogenes Club and we exited. Holmes dismissed the cab then strode towards the giant doors, I following behind. My visits to the club had been sporadic because it was not a joyful place to frequent. Holmes, I knew, spent long periods of time inside those eccentric walls because the environment allowed him to think undistracted. Once we entered through the heavy oak doors, a footman took us through those rooms where no member could speak nor take notice of any other, save in the Stranger's Room, which was our terminus.

We were directed into an anteroom where Holmes and the footman left me for several minutes. When Holmes returned, he gestured me to follow and we proceeded on to the Stranger's Room.

The room comprised high-backed chairs in huddled groups around an outer wall. If needed, it could certainly accommodate twenty people, but they would be spread apart, so as not to interfere with each other. Holmes took the grouping of chairs that faced a dining table, sat in front of a roaring open fireplace. To our right, large bay windows flooded the room with ample light.

'Now,' Holmes said, seated in an ancient red-leather chair. 'We will smoke and wait for our guests to arrive.'

Holmes planned the events of the day with his usual precision, even down to what we would eat for lunch. Inspector Bradstreet was the first to arrive, followed closely by Chief Inspector Mulgrave. Lunch came in, and we settled around the table. Mulgrave was the first to speak. I could tell by his posture he held no kindness towards Holmes.

'Perhaps you might explain why I am here. I am not accustomed to being summoned.'

Holmes poured him a glass of wine, and this did little to unsour his mood.

'It is time for us to become better acquainted,' he said, after pouring the rest of the bottle into our glasses. 'I assume you understand what prompted the invite?'

Bradstreet shifted in his chair, but said nothing. Mulgrave narrowed his eyes at Holmes, then took a sip of wine and shook his head.

'I cannot say I do,' he replied.

Holmes gave a snort and Mulgrave glared back at him. 'Very well. It's this Langsdale House business, isn't it?'

'Quite so,' Holmes said, sitting beside him. 'I know almost everything, Chief Inspector. Let us dispense then with threats and veiled subterfuges. It is time we lay the thing out in the open.'

'I'm not sure what Bradstreet has been telling you, but...'

Holmes put up a hand. 'Your reluctance forces my hand. It all started forty years ago with a murder-suicide at Langsdale House, am I correct?'

Bradstreet gave Holmes a shocked look, but Mulgrave simply chuckled.

'I must congratulate you, Mr Holmes,' the Chief Inspector remarked. 'I admit to being surprised by how deep you've looked into things. I cannot see why it is any business of yours.'

'You will forgive me, but it *is* my business,' Holmes replied.

'What can you know of it?'

'I know you were one of the attending constables.'

Mulgrave raised an eyebrow. 'Actually,' he said, putting down his glass and throwing a quick look at Bradstreet. 'I was *the* attending constable.'

Holmes smiled. 'You were the first official to arrive when the alarm was raised?'

The chief inspector nodded and relaxed his sour expression. 'It was my first call. Back then, the force was smaller than it is now. The station comprised four constables and Sergeant McGowen. He was ex-army. A Scotsman with a fiery temper. He had a hard reputation, Mr Holmes. McGowen was a drunkard. It wasn't just locals who stood terrified by his foul moods, especially if he'd been at the bottle, let me tell you.'

'Sergeant Birch was one of those four constables?'

Mulgrave nodded. 'We came through our training together. We were fresh with hardly any skills. I attended the house but realised quickly enough it was outside of my experience. I secured as much as I could, then sent a runner to get the others. It was late in the afternoon, so I knew McGowen would have already hit the bottle hard. Birch and I did our best, but McGowen, roaringly drunk, caused a terrible scene. It took both of us to convince him to let us take charge and by the time he had gone...'

'The weapon Colonel Harry Hodgkin-Tramwell had been holding had disappeared?'

'You speak as if you were there,' Mulgrave said.

'Who do you think took it?'

'We never found that out, although both Birch and I had our suspicions.'

'You suspected McGowen?' Holmes asked.

Mulgrave sighed. 'It was all impossible. We asked if he'd removed it and perhaps forgotten to tell us – he usually had little recollection of events after sobering up – but he flat out denied it. When we pushed, he became so difficult we let it go. What could we, being fresh with no experience, do? When an Inspector came, we handed over everything and explained we'd failed to find the gun.'

Holmes sat back in his chair. 'Thank you. Then came this current situation. I expect once Birch responded to that house again, and found circumstances similar, he immediately contacted you?'

'That's correct. What are the odds that a case so similar might happen again in that house? Birch secured things. I was engaged with another case and sent Bradstreet to begin the investigation for me.'

Our lunch was by now completed and we took seats in the comfortable old chairs.

Holmes then continued questioning Mulgrave.

'I mean no offence by saying this, Chief Inspector, but was it fear that the investigation might uncover yours and Birch's poor handling of the previous case which prompted your decision to close the current one?'

Mulgrave looked at Bradstreet for a moment, then turned to Holmes and shook his head.

'It crossed my mind, but no. I would never have forced Bradstreet to close the case based on the failings of the past. There was another reason.'

'What other reasons? Were you already investigating Langsdale House?'

He shifted in his chair. 'You seem to know everything, Mr Holmes.'

'It would be in your best interest to make a clean break of things.'

Mulgrave stood and stared out the window. With a sigh he turned and walked back to us. 'None of this is a reflection on you, Bradstreet. My orders came from high up the chain. You could not let it drop, could you?'

Bradstreet looked hard at him. 'There were too many concerns to let it drop, sir.'

'We might both come to regret that you didn't.'

Mulgrave sank back into his chair with a sigh.

Holmes lit his pipe. 'Let us turn to why that postulation was necessary.'

'Because of the brothel, I imagine?' Bradstreet said.

Mulgrave looked sharply at him. 'How could you know that?'

'How could I not? Your well-kept secret is nothing of the sort, *Chief* Inspector. I know nearly all the street girls from Hammersmith to South Kensington. My lads have been monitoring that house for weeks, with Birch's help.'

'Birch!' Mulgrave snarled. 'He has a lot to answer for. Only the superintendent and I were aware of things, or so I thought.'

Holmes blew out a puff of smoke over his head. 'One imagines the superintendent might come under pressure to have the case closed, once the evidence of Wallace's death hit the press?'

'Exactly right, Mr Holmes,' Mulgrave said, nodding. 'Wallace had several high-profile clients. It was a straightforward case of murder-suicide, requiring superficial investigation only. Wallace was still clutching the weapon. The witnesses heard a quarrel. There was no other evidence to suspect anything other than Wallace murdered Harold, then killed himself. Bradstreet then came by with his theories, and for the good of some significant people, I acted by closing the case.'

'It had too many unanswered questions,' Bradstreet growled.

'Theories are not facts, Inspector,' Mulgrave replied, lifting his head.

Holmes gave Bradstreet a look, and he fell back in his chair.

'Was it you, Chief Inspector, who set the dogs on me?' Holmes asked.

Mulgrave frowned. 'I know nothing about any dogs?'

'A band of men have dogged my investigation from the beginning. Two attacked me, their intention to murder me clear. After I had them under my boot, they confessed. They suggested you ordered things.'

Chief Inspector Mulgrave shook his head. 'I know nothing of it.'

'They seemed convinced by your involvement,' Holmes persisted.

'Accusations against senior police officers come with a heavy price, Mr Holmes.'

'Was that threat for me?'

Mulgrave's eyes darted between us all. 'To anyone, who might make such claims.'

Holmes rubbed his chin. 'Did you close the case of your own volition, or was it ordered by the superintendent?'

'The superintendent relayed his concerns, and I acted on them. I've been patient, but it's wearing thin.' There was a dangerous undercurrent to his statement.

Holmes seemed to ignore it. 'I will reward your patience, Chief Inspector. Did the superintendent know a brothel existed on the estate?'

'Yes, he was aware.'

'Was it yours or his concern that its discovery would cause public scandal to any client members of higher status, specifically to those men who frequented and availed themselves of its services?'

'His.'

'Did it not occur to you that those whom you considered being incommoded by an investigation should actually *be* the subject of one themselves?'

Mulgrave laughed. 'Be reasonable, Mr Holmes. How could I? The superintendent forced my hand. He is a dangerous man, especially to those he considers his enemies. Believe me.'

'That is odd, Chief Inspector,' remarked Holmes. 'I've always found Peterson to be a fair-minded champion of the law.'

Mulgrave threw him a terrible look. 'You don't know him like I do.'

Inspector Bradstreet stood. 'I agree with Mr Holmes. Superintendent Peterson has always been fair and consistent with me.'

Mulgrave stared up at him. 'Look, both of you, there's no point in going any further with these enquires. You must let them drop.'

'Why? Because the superintendent will not recognise his supposed involvement in this case?'

Mulgrave now stood. 'Peterson will say nothing, I can assure you. If you both persist with this, I'll take actions neither of you will care for. Drop it, or I'll drop you.'

'Is that so?' A strong commanding voice said from somewhere further into the room.

We turned to witness a tall man, along with three others – one of whom was the rotund Mycroft Holmes – rising from their high-backed chairs which hid them.

The four men came beside us. The colour drained from Mulgrave's face as he backed away.

'I took the liberty of inviting Superintendent Peterson, who has been quietly listening in on our brief conversation. I hope it hasn't caused you any inconvenience, *Chief* Inspector?'

'Curse you,' Mulgrave said. He attempted to flee, but found the way blocked by two men who were standing in front of the door. Inspector Bradstreet grabbed him by the arm, forcing him back to the table. Superintendent Peterson pulled a chair out and pointed to it.

'Sit there and don't say another word.'

Chief Inspector Mulgrave sat as instructed.

Mycroft came and stood alongside me.

'Now,' Holmes said to Mulgrave, who was being flanked by Inspector Bradstreet and Superintendent Peterson. 'Perhaps we might go over the details of the Langsdale House brothel that you appear to have a hand in running?'

There was little more to be discovered. Chief Inspector Mulgrave refused to answer any of Holmes's follow-up questions. Eventually, Superintendent Peterson arrested

Mulgrave, and those two other men took him away to Scotland Yard.

'A nasty business, Mr Holmes,' said Peterson as he watched Mulgrave marched away. 'You think Mulgrave was running this brothel?'

'No, he hasn't the brains for it.'

'In the meantime, we will do what we can to find his accomplices. I'll have men over there today, to shut it all down.'

Holmes shook his head. 'With your permission, I ask you let me handle the details. It would upset my plans to have the police at Langsdale now.'

Peterson turned to Bradstreet. 'It's irregular. What do you say, Inspector?'

'I trust Mr Holmes, sir. I am inclined to listen to what he has to say.'

The superintendent nodded. 'I'll expect a report soon, Inspector.'

With the superintendent now gone, we all relaxed.

'The distraction of this brothel business is over,' Holmes said. 'We are free to spend our time contemplating the real crime.'

'Which is what, exactly?' Bradstreet asked.

'The deaths of three people at Langsdale House.'

'Grim. But three?' Inspector Bradstreet said, frowning. 'I count only two.'

I turned to Bradstreet. 'There is the missing prostitute, Elsie. We think she died on the estate too.'

'If we are to consider Elsie,' Holmes remarked. 'I might amend my count to four.'

'Well,' Mycroft Holmes said. 'This entire escapade has been altogether far *too* exciting. It has upset my constitution. Sherlock, I will take my leave.'

Chapter Ten

There comes a time when every boy must eventually grow up

Inspector Bradstreet and I listened as Holmes laid out the next moves in bringing our case to its conclusion. Holmes gave away little, electing to explain only what he felt necessary for us to prepare for. I could tell from Holmes's inaction there must have been something missing from his evidence to wrap the case up. Some small bit of data, a last clue, perhaps, that would make his solution complete.

'You each know what I require?'

We both nodded.

Bradstreet stood. 'Bring enough men to secure the house and wait for you and the doctor before we enter. I'll be there at the right time, but why can't you tell me anything about it now?'

'Things must unravel at their own pace. You know my methods, Bradstreet.'

The inspector chuckled. 'I've known you long enough. You've always played things close to your chest. Fine, I'll have the men ready. Is there anything else you need me to arrange before this evening?'

Holmes shook his head. 'There are one or two things I must do in order to complete my case. You have my instructions. I will see you tonight.'

'Till tonight then.' Inspector Bradstreet then left.

Holmes turned to me. 'Now we head to the endgame. I want you to go to Baker Street. I am expecting Harmony to call, and would like you there to greet her.'

'You can count on me, but what of you?'

'There are loose ends I need to deal with. It will be quicker alone. Have yourself readied to leave by eight. Should I not return by then, proceed to Langsdale House as agreed, and bring Harmony with you. We will need her help before the night is out. Oh, and Watson,' he said, his expression turning grim. 'Bring your revolver.'

*

It had been a restless hour or two, waiting for Holmes to return. I must have consumed an entire pot of coffee and smoked two cigars in my unrest. When I heard our bell ringing, my heart jumped with joy. Knowing Holmes would have used his key, I deduced, correctly, it was Harmony who called. I rushed to the door and opened it, relieved to see Lady Harmony chatting with Mrs Hudson on the stair. She looked regal in a stunning, fashionable blue dress. It was a far different lady from Harry who now entered the house.

Mrs Hudson laughed as they came up to greet me.

'*Lady* Harmony Brady is here to see you, Doctor.'

Harmony smiled at Mrs Hudson, who then left us alone.

'Good to see you again, John. You don't mind if I call you that?'

'No,' I replied. 'Please, sit and let me get you a drink of something. Tea?'

'Do you have anything stronger,' she asked, rubbing her forehead and sitting in a chair beside the fire. 'It has been a very trying few days.'

'Of course,' I said. 'A whiskey soda, perhaps?'

'Please.'

I poured us both a glass and sat opposite her.

'So, what can you tell me of your exploits?'

Harmony took a sip of her drink and sighed. 'That's much better. What can I say that you don't already know? The lust of men over helpless women remains as despicable as ever. As you know, I spent several days undercover as a street girl working for a man named Barny "Brains" Simpson. It was through him I found myself at Langsdale House. Brains, who does not live up to his nickname, has several girls. Their clients mostly comprise the higher classes. The house has a roving group of six rough men, who all take a turn with those poor girls when the fancy takes them.

'Those living at Langsdale are young, no older than twenty. They are treated better than if they were on the street, but not by those who pay for their services, and certainly not by the men paid to protect them. It's a terrible place, John. The house is in a shocking state, but the girls made the rooms nice. Clients come mostly at night. I made myself indispensable to Brains. Over time, he came to trust me enough to let me manage things, and he put me to work getting those girls clean and groomed. Now Wallace is no longer with them, Brains had a new doctor check them regularly. It might surprise you to learn Wallace apparently never touched the girls. His stepson, well, that's a different story entirely. He apparently had a bit of a thing for the younger ones, and his wants were a little beyond what they expected.

'They earn very little, because what money they get comes after expenses are taken to cover food and living. In the last few days, we've seen fewer clients. It caused several girls to head back out onto the street.'

'Did you see any of the house staff? Mr Dawson perhaps?'

'Yes, old Dawson came pretty regularly, although not for any other reason than to escape from his wife. *She* is an interesting character. According to one of the longest serving girls, Mrs Dawson has not set foot in the annex the entire time she's been at the house. She collects the rent money every

Friday at noon and always stands some distance away. I suspect she dislikes what is going on, but counts the money anyway – and it generates a considerable sum. Aside from those really important clients, Brains has a club for people with money to spare, which they all pitch into weekly. Some come more frequently than others. There was a bit of a to-do a fortnight back. Patty Smith said they're treated pretty well, whatever that means, as long as they didn't break the golden rule. I suppose, given the secrecy involved, Brains has a hard line with girls who take on clients outside of the house. Seems one of them broke this rule, and they quickly dismissed her.'

'Was her name Elsie?' I asked, hoping to be wrong.

'Yes, that *was* her name. But how did you know?'

I sighed, then gave her a brief explanation, leaving out any names.

'How awful. I have to say, John, despite the rough treatment these girls sometimes endure, I saw no evidence they suffered beyond losing money and maybe a little food. The girls were lucky that Brains also had a rule about violence, and the men who worked for him understood they'd lose their privileges if they put a hand on them. As I said before, it's a nasty place, but most of those girls chose to be there and could leave at any time. Brains had enough waiting to replace them.'

'What about drugs?'

She shook her head. 'Brains won't allow it. The house is clean, surprisingly.'

'Were the clients subject to similar rules?'

'Oh, yes. I can't say for certain the high-profile clients always followed them. But those men in the club would find themselves cut off for periods at a time. Repeat offenders were not treated with any kindness by the violent men who worked there. I heard they banned one of their more frequent club clients, I don't recall his name, after the whole Elsie incident.'

'That certainly must have done a lot to secure the safety of these girls?'

Harmony smiled at me. 'Very much so. I wish I could recall his name. He's a greengrocer in Covent Garden. Supplied the house with most of the fruit and vegetables. I was told the hullabaloo involved his son. When Brains found out, it caused a real brouhaha.'

'His name is Popplewick. It answers the question why he refused to allow his son to marry her, and also why he was insistent Elsie continued coming to the house,' I said, trying hard to keep the level of disgust in my voice from turning to anger.

'His boy has fallen for her, is that it? And the father allowed her to stay in his house, knowing who and what she was?'

'He apparently gave her a separate room.'

Harmony shook her head. 'That explains why Brains banned him, and why Elsie was put back on the street. What an odious thing for a father to do to his own child. Did the boy know?'

'I don't think so. As far as he's concerned, she went missing. He came to ask me to convince Holmes to find her. He initially refused, which I admit maddened me, but I have since come to understand why. We think she was murdered.'

Harmony looked shocked. 'Why do you think that?'

'Holmes and I discovered a body in the morgue, badly burnt, and all indications suggest it was hers.'

'How long ago was this?'

'Around a week or so? I can't say for certain when she died, but it must have been within that period or the decomposition would have been greater.'

'I always imagined burning to be a horrible way to die.'

I had no adequate response, so steered the conversation away.

'This Brains fellow, he runs the day-to-day business, but is not the actual brains, is he? What part did Chief Inspector Mulgrave play in it?'

'I don't know, but they all fear the chief inspector. The rumour is, he took a percentage to keep it all secret, you know, so no officials poked their noses in. Langsdale had clients from all over, including positions of government. One girl told me about a visit from some posh-knob, and his visits increased in frequency after Wallace died. That can't be a coincidence. I don't know who he was, but the girls said when he came, he always acted like he owned the place. Maybe he did? This morning things came to a head when I saw old Dawson on my way up. He said they'd shut things down and cleared out.'

'Mulgrave most probably alerted them. Did you know the superintendent arrested him this afternoon?'

'I did not. Well, that would do it,' she said.

Harmony and I looked up as the clock chimed the hour.

'Six,' Harmony said with a huff. 'I see Mr Holmes still has no grasp of punctuality.'

'Not unless it suits him to be punctual,' I replied. 'It's not that unusual, really. If you are willing, I suggest we dine here, then make preparations for our trip to Langsdale House. A cab will be here around eight.'

Lady Harmony smiled. 'I would like that, John. Very much. Are you sure we should go without Mr Holmes?'

'He gave explicit instruction in that regard.'

After Mrs Hudson had served us dinner, Harmony and I sat beside the fire and talked. Lost in the ebb and flow of our conversations, it startled us to hear the chime of the clock as it struck the hour of eight. We scrambled to get everything we needed. Mrs Hudson let us know a cab was waiting and we descended. When I opened the door to allow Harmony to enter, Holmes was sitting inside with young Mr Popplewick. Once we had settled, the cabman flicked the reins and we moved off.

'Lady Harmony, this is Mr Popplewick,' Holmes said. The boy shook hands with her. 'Watson, you already know,' he remarked.

'Yes indeed,' he said, energetically shaking my hand too. Popplewick's inclusion felt cruel, given that his demeanour suggested Holmes had given no indication what he believed had become of Elsie.

'It surprises me,' I remarked, my eyes set firmly on Holmes. 'I thought you engaged on *other* business.'

'No, my dear Watson. It is to you that we must both be thankful. I had not given Mr Popplewick the attention he deserved, especially after your impassioned plea.'

'I do hope we haven't asked My Popplewick here only to disappoint and possibly cause him undue emotional distress?'

Young Popplewick leant forwards in his chair. 'No matter what we discover, I have to know.'

'There you are, dear Watson, all is well. Besides,' he said, his expression hardening, 'there comes a time when every boy must eventually grow up, wouldn't you agree?'

I sat back in my chair and looked out the window. Harmony, who had said little, patted my hand. We made the rest of the journey in silence. When the cab pulled into the lane leading to the house, Holmes tapped the ceiling of our carriage and the cab came to a halt.

We all exited and watched Holmes talk softly with the driver who then stepped away as the horses were steered away.

'The cab will wait for us. We will walk the rest of the way.' Holmes then strode off towards the house.

There was movement up ahead. I drew Holmes's attention to it.

'It's Bradstreet,' he said in response. 'The game, my dear fellow, is afoot. Come on.'

Chapter Eleven

What an entirely grotesque affair

We met with Inspector Bradstreet and a cadre of ten uni-
formed officers in the overgrowth ahead. The strange way the
moonlight reflected off my friend's eyes, and his tight posture,
told me he was expecting trouble.

'What's the plan?' Bradstreet said.

'A frontal assault,' replied Holmes. 'Have half your men
remain back.'

Bradstreet gave his orders to the officers and then returned
next to us.

Holmes pulled out a revolver, as did I. Bradstreet eyed us
both. 'What exactly are we walking into?'

'Danger. Are you armed?'

Bradstreet pulled out a pistol of his own. 'I hope I don't
need to use it.'

'The threat is clear and present, Inspector,' Holmes said,
checking his weapon. 'We may meet resistance, but with good
fortune,' he said, brandishing his revolver, 'these should
mitigate against a prolonged fight.'

'Provided they aren't also armed,' Bradstreet muttered.

Holmes ignored him and turned to us.

'Watson and I will take the lead. Bradstreet will follow, backed by his officers. Harmony and Popplewick, remain behind them. Enter only when it seems safe to do so.'

'You worry about yourself,' Harmony replied. 'I'll take care of the boy.'

Holmes gave us a smile. 'We are ready?'

'Lead on,' Bradstreet said.

Holmes kept a brisk pace, and it wasn't long before we emerged near the shabby lawn. We could now see the front door, which stood open. Holmes put a hand out and stopped us from going further.

'It's murder. Come, all of you, into the house!'

We followed Holmes as he burst ahead and just as I was about to cross the threshold, he stopped and threw out his long arm, pointing to the floor.

'Look,' he said. 'Footmarks, fresh wet footmarks. Have we arrived too late?'

It was at that point five rough-looking men burst from a closed door to engage us, with Mrs Dawson behind them. The men came armed with either what they had on them, or what they'd found to hand. For a moment they faltered at the sight of our superior firearms.

'That's far enough,' Holmes said, covering the group with his revolver. 'The game is up.'

Inspector Bradstreet and his officers stepped forwards and all five men scrambled away. What followed was a chase around the house. Some escaped, but soon found themselves overwhelmed by the officers waiting outside. I rushed to Holmes, who was engaged in a struggle with a brute of a man, who looked likely to murder him. A blow from my revolver to the back of his head saw him stagger back and two officers descended on him. It wasn't long after that he and his compatriots were all handcuffed and seated on the floor.

Mrs Dawson attempted to flee, but met her match in Harmony and Popplewick, who dragged her back into the foyer, cursing and yelling.

Once Bradstreet had accounted for everyone, he blew a whistle, and two police carts arrived at the front door. All five men were then imprisoned inside, leaving only Mrs Dawson to face us. A constable slapped a pair of irons on her.

'Bradstreet can keep order down here,' Holmes said, as Harmony joined us by the stair. 'Follow me, both of you, and pray we are not too late!'

Holmes leapt up the stairs, two or three at a time, with Harmony and I following closely behind. He ran along the landing to the door of Mrs Houston-Smythe's room and tried it.

'Locked,' he cursed.

'I'll get the keys,' I said, but Holmes shook his head.

'There is no time, put your shoulder to it.'

On the count of three, we both hit the door. It took several attempts, but eventually the door gave to our assault. Holmes and I staggered in with Harmony behind us.

The room was in complete darkness. Holmes struck a match and moved to a table, lighting a heavy green candle. We then lit the remaining candles and when the light filled the room, we spotted the heavily veiled woman lying prone on her bed.

Holmes leapt to the bed. 'Doctor, your services are needed.'

I approached and turned her, feeling for a pulse. It was weak, but it was there.

'She's alive,' I said.

I heard Holmes's sigh of relief.

'Who is she?' Harmony asked.

'Mrs Houston-Smythe,' I responded.

Holmes shook his head. 'I think not. Check again.'

I pulled the veil from her face and was surprised to see a far younger woman hidden underneath. I looked back at Holmes and frowned.

'Elsie,' he said. 'Popplewick's girl.'

My mouth dropped as I turned back to her. 'Then whose

body did we see at the morgue?'

'It was Mrs Houston-Smythe,' Holmes replied. 'Will Elsie recover?'

'Bring your candle closer,' I said. I made a brief examination. 'She's unconscious. With such a weak pulse, she could have been drugged?' As I ministered to her, a thought occurred, and I looked at Holmes. 'Chloral hydrate?'

Holmes picked up a half-full glass of water from the bedside cabinet and sniffed it.

'I concur, and almost certainly delivered in this glass.'

'We have no time to lose.' I removed my jacket then opened my bag. 'We must empty her stomach. Harmony, there is a bathroom along this corridor. Get me a pitcher of water and a chamber pot, quickly.'

Holmes assisted me with my apparatus as I began preparing Elsie for the procedure. When Harmony returned, I emptied Elsie's stomach.

'Will she survive, Watson?' Holmes asked.

'The odds are fifty-fifty,' I replied. 'Without knowing how much they dosed her with, or how long ago she consumed it, all we can do is wait, and hope. She needs to be in hospital.'

'Then we will ensure she gets the treatment she needs.' Holmes turned to Harmony. 'Would you remain here with Elsie?'

'Of course,' Harmony said. 'Send the boy up. If Elsie isn't to survive, he can at least hold her hand.'

Holmes nodded. 'Doctor, come. I suspect there will be need of your services for another.'

Harmony sat beside Elsie and Holmes led me out.

'How long have you known Elsie has been impersonating Mrs Houston-Smythe?' I asked, feeling slightly put out he had let me go on believing Elsie was dead.

'The last pieces of the puzzle came together this morning.'

That made me feel a little better. 'We should explain things to Popplewick.'

'Harmony can do that.'

There was a shout and Holmes put a hand on my shoulder.

'Bradstreet. Given its distress, I fear it cannot be good.'

We ran to Bradstreet's call and found him in a lower bathroom at the end of a corridor, next to the kitchen. He and a constable were tending to Mr Dawson, who was naked and face down in a bath of water. Once Dawson was no longer in danger, Bradstreet beckoned for me to examine him.

'He's alive,' I said, over my shoulder. 'From the smell of him, I'd say both drunk and drugged. Luckily, he vomited into the water.' I pulled the plug and watched the water drain away.

'Let's get him out of this bath.'

It took four of us to lift Mr Dawson out onto the blankets a constable had laid for us. I shifted him to his side, and we covered him.

'I suspect he'll recover. His odds are better than Elsie's.'

'Elsie?' Bradstreet asked.

'All in good time, Inspector. Have a man stationed here and send one up the stairs as well. As soon as Mr Dawson recovers, let him dress and arrest him.'

'On what charge?'

'Conspiracy to commit murder will do for the moment.'

Bradstreet growled. 'I hope you're going to explain things soon, Mr Holmes.'

'There is no time like the present.'

With Mr Dawson being cared for, we headed to the front of the house. Mrs Dawson stood flanked by a constable.

Holmes turned to Popplewick, who had been standing to one side. 'Go upstairs, follow the corridor left, and find Harmony. Be strong,' he said, squeezing his shoulder. 'I suspect you have a long night ahead of you.'

I smiled as I watched Popplewick head up the stairs.

Holmes then turned his attention to Mrs Dawson.

'Good evening, madam,' he said. 'It will undoubtably disappoint you to know that despite your efforts to drown Mr Dawson, you failed. He will recover.'

'He remains a bitter disappointment,' she said with a sigh.

'I suspect once he recovers fully, he will be cooperative.'

She chuckled. 'I doubt it. He can barely remember his name most days. Tell me, who are you?'

'I am Sherlock Holmes, perhaps you have heard of me?'

Mrs Dawson sighed. 'Sherlock Holmes. They warned me about you a while back. You're the amateur detective.'

'Consulting detective, madam.'

'I have you to thank for all this?'

'You do, madam.'

She was thoughtful for a moment. 'You appear to have the cards stacked against me, Mr Holmes. Might I ask you to consider removing these restraints? I am no threat. I promise I'll not attempt to escape.'

Holmes nodded to the constable, who removed her cuffs.

'Thank you. Perhaps we might move to a more comfortable location?'

She took Holmes by the arm and led us to a furnished room, where we all sat. Mrs Dawson then looked at Bradstreet.

'May I know what am I being charged with?'

'Conspiracy to commit murder,' he said.

She laughed. 'Interesting.'

Holmes pulled out his cigarette case and offered her one, and they shared a match.

'Inspector, may I introduce Mrs Clara Hodgkin-Tramwell, the wife of the late Cecil Hodgkin-Tramwell who died, if you recall, in America approximately six years ago.'

'I am impressed, Mr Holmes. It is true.'

Inspector Bradstreet and I exchanged surprised looks.

'Wait a minute,' Bradstreet said. 'She died, it's a matter of public record.'

Mrs Dawson rolled her eyes. 'Inspector, it's probably best if Mr Holmes does the talking.'

Bradstreet growled, but Holmes held up a hand.

'Holmes,' she said. 'May I ask what you consider the charges against me to be?

'I thought we would start with the murder of Harold Houston, Doctor Wallace Houston-Smythe, and Mrs Houston-Smythe, and take it from there. But before we go any further. Inspector, please explain to Mrs Dawson her legal rights.'

Inspector Bradstreet nodded and proceeded as Holmes asked.

'Now,' Holmes said, rubbing his hands together. 'Shall we begin?'

'I can't decide if you're clever or just conceited, Mr Holmes.'

'A little of both,' he replied.

'Touché. May I be bold and ask how you learnt what I thought was undiscoverable?'

Holmes blew out a cloud of smoke. 'The case presented some difficulty. Once I had a full copy of the New Jersey coroner's records, which the American embassy was kind enough to supply, it became clear. As is so often the case in accidents on water, not all the bodies are recovered. Cecil Hodgkin-Tramwell's body was found, but his wife's wasn't. Although the verdict applied to you both, it suggested you may have survived.'

'Obviously, I did. Do you know why I went to all this trouble?'

'Because of an arrangement you made with Marjorie Houston-Smythe, or as you knew her before her first marriage, Marjorie Hodgkin-Tramwell. Your husband's sister, I believe?'

Mrs Dawson gasped. 'Now you really are something. How could you possibly know? Cecil's sister left for America when she was eleven. No one in this house knew anything about her.'

'It was in a police report on the death of Colonel and Mrs Patricia Hodgkin-Tramwell. Your husband's parents, I believe?'

She said nothing.

'When Watson read in the report that testimonies were gathered from the domestics, and their children, I pondered on whose children the report referenced. The domestics? Or the colonel and his wife? I admit I had no data to qualify why I thought the later, but your confirmation has now supplied it.'

This revelation surprised not only Mrs Dawson, but also

me, as I'd assumed the children referred to in the report were those of the domestics.

Mrs Dawson continued to remain quiet.

'Silence won't save you. Your only hope is to tell me everything. It will go badly for you, if you don't.'

'It is not a manly thing to browbeat a woman, Mr Holmes.'

'There have been three murders, madam. Two of which I can conclusively attribute to you.'

'I can see it is useless to hide anything from you. Very well. I will tell my story. This house and the estate had fallen into ill repair when I met my husband. He already had mounting debts, and the bank would extend no loans to either of us. We started this rumour we liked to travel. It's a small place, word like that spreads quickly enough. We let a few gossips know we often travelled to the Americas, when the truth was—'

'You were creating new personas for yourselves in Ireland?' Holmes asked, interrupting her.

Mrs Dawson raised an eyebrow. 'You are clever! Yes, once we'd established ourselves, we set sail for New Jersey, where Cecil's sister had been living for the last forty years. It was a simple plan, really. We intended to fake our deaths and start a new life in Ireland, as you said. With help from Marjorie, we planned to return after a short period had elapsed, to reclaim our house free from its debt.'

Holmes put out his cigarette. 'But that plan came undone when, rather ironically, the boat which you planned to disappear from, hit another, causing both to sink and your husband's actual death, correct?'

Mrs Dawson nodded. 'What a turn of events? After Cecil's death, I wanted to give the whole idea up, but Marjorie convinced me to go on with it. So, with news of our deaths officially reported to the British authorities, Marjorie continued Cecil's plan. She contacted the British Embassy who validated her claim on my estate. With a little trickery, Cecil and I had managed to obtain a loan through an American bank. It wasn't as hard as you might think. Once we were declared dead the responsibility for those loans died with us. I gave almost all of it to Marjorie, keeping a little back for my own needs, so she could pay off the estate death duties and move ahead with her inheritance claim. You're probably wondering why I didn't just pay them off myself? Well, when we were considered dead, the outstanding debts on the house including our existing bank loans, were cleared. Marjorie's cost for the estate was much easier to settle. I travelled to Ireland as agreed, and started my new life. Not long after I met Dawson and we married. It was not for love, you understand. It was a business arrangement I concocted to foil the unfair ridiculousness of our society. A woman is not entitled to the same privileges as a man in England. I kept him in booze and that's all he cared about. Marjorie communicated with me regularly and things continued just fine until she married that loathsome Wallace.'

Mrs Dawson put her cigarette out and went to a small table and poured herself a brandy.

'I suppose Marjorie had become used to the idea of owning this house, so she changed things. When communication stopped, I suspected something amiss. I packed up Dawson and we arrived soon after. That was when I confirmed my suspicions. She, Wallace, and Harold sat me down in this room. That hateful boy then told me they'd made a legal change so he would own my estate. Can you believe that? And, since he knew I could explain none of it to the police, there was little I could do. But I am no fool, Mr Holmes. I played along with their game.'

'And that was when you came up with a method to resolve things in your favour?' Holmes asked.

'Not right away. Marjorie still held a lot of sadness over the death of her brother, and found me, in that regard, a sympathetic companion. I put up with her boy and husband. I had all but given up the idea of seeking any kind of retribution, until I discovered Wallace and his brother, along with that disgusting boy, were running a brothel here. From that moment on, Mr Holmes, my mind turned to how I could get rid of them all. The obstacle was the boy. I manoeuvred Marjorie into telling me how and when the legal transfer to

Harold would occur. Cecil had spoken on and off about how his parents had died. He had never recovered from it, truthfully.'

'It was the murder and suicide of Cecil's parents which gave you the idea?'

She nodded. 'But then something happened, which made me pause.'

Holmes pulled out his pipe and lit it.

'Harold contracted syphilis.'

'Exactly. Despite Wallace's ministrations, he couldn't cure the boy. You cannot imagine how happy I was. Perhaps God would take care of the problem for me? But he didn't. That hateful boy clung on, and on, and with his birthday coming, well, my options were running out. I had to act.'

'That was when you met Barny Simpson?'

Mrs Dawson smiled. 'Yes. Harold collected rent from that vile brothel, but as his condition worsened, he could no longer leave the house. At Marjorie's urging, I began collecting it for her. Barny Simpson was not what I expected. He's actually a fair man, for a ruffian, but like many of his class, he has contacts with those who are not so friendly.'

Holmes let a cloud of smoke flow over his head. 'You befriended Barny Simpson?'

She shrugged. 'You could say I struck up a friendship with the man. Despite everything, he seemed trustworthy enough. Once he knew my situation and what it might mean to him personally, it wasn't hard to convince him to fall in with my plans.'

'How did you coerce him?'

'With money, Mr Holmes. It's the easiest way. Barny suggested we take care of Marjorie first.'

'With Elsie set to impersonate her?'

She nodded. 'Elsie owed Simpson. She wasn't difficult to persuade either.'

'But this substitution could not have worked for long, as Wallace would have discovered it almost immediately.'

'He and Marjorie had a very close relationship. Our plans

moved quickly once Marjorie was dead.'

Mrs Dawson rubbed her eyes.

Holmes then took up the story.

'This is how I believe it happened and please stop me if I have any details incorrect. You drugged Harold and Wallace with chloral hydrate, which they succumbed to quickly. You put it in the jam, since Harold, I gather, preferred to eat it right from the jar. He was the first to become incapacitated, as he had ingested a higher amount. Wallace went to assist him, but he too succumbed to its effects.'

Mrs Dawson smiled. 'I put it into the orange juice as well, as I could not be sure Wallace would eat the jam.'

Holmes inclined his head. 'Wallace, however, remained somewhat alert enough to fall against the table, where his left hand became coated in jam. He took a spoon, perhaps to use it against you. Simpson's men put Wallace upstairs, then placed Harold downstairs. You took a pistol and shot Wallace through the right side of his head. You then went to Harold's room and shot him too. Afterwards, you returned to Wallace and placed the gun in his right hand.'

Mrs Dawson gasped. 'How could you know all that?'

'Was any detail incorrect?'

Mrs Dawson shook her head. 'You left out one thing. After Harold was dead, we discovered he still had jam in his mouth. No one wanted to touch him to get it out, because of his condition, so we put the jam next to him. We thought it might look like he had been eating it when he was shot.'

'Ingenious, but you made three serious mistakes.'

'The spoon?'

'Exactly. Had you put that spoon by the jar next to Harold, it might not have raised questions.'

She sighed. 'I only considered it once the inspector here asked about it. Wallace had it all along and we didn't notice.'

'We might have overlooked that mistake, had you not placed the gun into Wallace's right hand. Since he was left-handed, it cast serious doubt upon the claim of suicide.'

Mrs Dawson shook her head. 'Yes. Such a silly mistake.'

'Your third was defiantly the worst,' he said.

She frowned. 'What was it?'

The expression on Holmes's face turned hard. 'Failing to take seriously the warnings you received regarding me.'

Mrs Dawson let out a snort-laugh. 'A mistake, I suspect, others have made at their cost. You're a wizard.'

'No, madam,' he replied, sitting back into his chair. 'I am simply a good detective. Inspector Bradstreet, we have heard all we needed from Mrs Dawson. You may take her away.'

Inspector Bradstreet organised for Mr Dawson and Elsie to be transported to hospital. Lady Harmony and Mr Popplewick went with Elsie, and all the men who'd been arrested at the house were taken to Scotland Yard.

Holmes and I sat smoking in the room we'd heard Mrs Dawson's confession in. There were several constables in the house and its grounds. It wasn't long before Inspector Bradstreet joined us.

'My men are conducting a search of the place now,' he said, sitting down heavily into the chair. 'Simpson could be hiding out somewhere on the property.'

'Unlikely, but it is better to be sure,' Holmes said.

'I also have men looking in a few known hideouts. We'll catch him,' Bradstreet said.

'He's gone to ground. Simpson committed murder and he knows what that brings. I very much doubt you will find him.'

'We know a lot of the usual hiding places these men bolt to,' Bradstreet said. 'It might take us a bit of time, but we'll flush him out.'

'Bradstreet, Simpson has reason to stay hidden. It will be an arduous task catching him. I do not doubt your tenacity, but there may be another option, if you are willing to hear it?'

Bradstreet sighed. 'Aye, I'm willing?'

'Pull your men off the hunt and I'll set the irregulars on him.'

'Those street urchins of yours? I don't know.'

Holmes smiled. 'They can infiltrate into places your men

could never hope to go. If he's in London, the irregulars will find him.'

Bradstreet thought for a moment, then nodded. 'I'll leave that to you then. You're absolutely sure Simpson murdered Mrs Houston-Smythe?'

'The violence used was consistent with Simpson, and we also have Mrs Dawson's confession to corroborate it.'

'And you're positive Mrs Dawson killed the other two?'

Holmes smiled. 'The spilt wax proved she did it.'

'Spilt wax?' Bradstreet said, frowning. 'What are you talking about?'

'When Mrs Dawson killed Wallace, he fell against the table knocking a candle over. It had been lit for approximately thirty minutes. A quantity of wax split on the floor, which she inadvertently stepped in. Without knowing it, she transferred that wax into Harold's room. It was how I could determine the correct sequence of their deaths.'

'That was why you performed those experiments in the street?' I asked. 'And why you pretended to fall when we first met her. You needed to examine her shoes!'

Holmes beamed. 'Correct. I had ruled Mr Dawson out by that point. It led me to consider his wife. When I fell and examined her shoe, I noticed at once a quantity of that hardened green wax still visible on the side and sole. There was wax on the stairs, which Mrs Dawson had transferred from Wallace's room. I know this because the trace diminished in size with each step away from it. My experiment proved the time the wax took to harden and duplicated the diminishing size of each trace as I walked through it.'

Bradstreet laughed. 'Wax traces are all fine, in theories. I'll be far happier once Simpson is in custody.'

'Won't it be difficult to prove she actually fired the shots that killed them?' I asked.

Holmes turned to me. 'That falls in the jury's purview. All I can do is supply the evidence and leave the rest to you, Inspector.'

'Hold on a minute,' I said. 'There's something else I just

considered. The jam. When I suggested the jam may have been used to mask Harold's syphilis treatment, you gave the impression I was correct.'

Holmes chuckled. 'I admit I gave that impression whilst I considered it.'

I folded my arms. 'When did you decide there was a different answer?'

'After I'd determined the true reason Wallace held onto that spoon. Your idea of concealment, however unlikely, might have been correct had Wallace killed Harold.'

'I see,' I said, a little disgruntled. 'Harold simply fell unconscious whilst eating it?'

Holmes raised an eyebrow. 'Falling unconscious whilst eating jam is a far less fanciful idea than someone pushing a spoonful into a dead man's mouth. Would you not agree?'

'Yes,' I said, chuckling. 'When you put it like that, it does seem more plausible.'

'Well, of course it is,' Holmes said.

Despite the disappointment of discovering my theory was not correct, I had to admit the entire jam business was comical.

'There's one thing I don't fully understand,' Bradstreet said. 'What was Mrs Dawson's motive in killing them all? Was it revenge for breaking the agreement?'

Holmes smiled. 'Harold Houston's greed sealed all their fates when he robbed her of her estate by making those legal changes. Of course, once Harold was dead, it meant Marjorie Houston-Smythe would keep ownership of the estate. It might have been possible that Marjorie would hand it over when her son and husband were dead. I suspect Mrs Dawson's hatefulness had taken her too far to even consider the possibility. Marjorie had to die. Killing her first was, perhaps, a kindness, as she would not have to see her son dead.'

'And Elsie and Mr Dawson,' I asked. 'What would be the explanation had we not saved them?'

'Elsie's impersonation was necessary to maintain the illusion Marjorie was still alive. I surmise Mrs Dawson faked Marjorie's will, which would leave the estate to her. It would appear Mr Dawson, a known drunkard, had fallen unconscious from drink in the bath and drowned. Marjorie would probably take her own life, with Elsie's body rendered unidentifiable to perpetuate the illusion beyond her death.'

'Mrs Dawson got all this from the murder-suicide of her husband's parents?' Bradstreet asked.

I nodded. 'It is a terribly sad affair.'

'Sickening, I'd say. Do you think we'll ever know if the other two from that previous case were murdered?' Bradstreet asked.

Holmes shrugged. 'Doubtful. The verdict in that case appears legitimate, and with no way of undoing it, we must leave it at that. Well, Bradstreet. I think it is time for Watson and I to let you get on with your work.'

Once we'd said our goodbyes, we took our cab home to Baker Street.

'What do you think will happen to Elsie?'

Holmes sighed. 'She has some hard questions to answer for, but we might make a case to explain things. Elsie was an unwilling participant, but she almost certainly understood why she was impersonating Mrs Houston-Smythe. She will have to answer for that. Barny Simpson's confession will aide her, provided he is caught. I cannot say how much, but at the very least it should lessen her sentence.'

'Will she see time behind bars?'

'I think it likely,' Holmes said. 'Whatever the outcome, I suspect Elsie will have a new life waiting for her in young Mr Popplewick.'

'What an entirely grotesque affair,' I remarked, shaking my head.

'A grotesque affair indeed,' agreed Holmes.

Epilogue

Despite Inspector Bradstreet's reservations, the irregulars found Barny Simpson hiding out in the East End of London. He was arrested and charged with Marjorie Houston-Smythe's murder, and the case went to court a month after. Holmes and Bradstreet worked long hours putting their case-notes in order. They placed enough evidence forwards to ensure a tight case against them, but Mrs Dawson's defence lawyer managed to cast enough doubt over his client's participation, that the judge felt it was impossible to prove beyond all reasonable doubt that she pulled the trigger in both cases. Nevertheless, Mrs Dawson was tried along with Mr Dawson, Barny Simpson, and Elise Barlow, on the charges of murder and conspiracy to commit murder. Once all the evidence was taken into consideration, they were each found guilty.

Mrs Dawson was handed life imprisonment.

Mr Dawson was fortunate to take a custodial sentence of eight months, as he was proven to be an unwilling conspirator.

They sentenced Barny Simpson to execution for the murder of Marjorie, with an option to appeal.

Elsie Barlow was finally handed a custodial sentence of three months, which came after Holmes entered an impassioned plea on her behalf. Mr Popplewick remained by her side throughout the entire trial, and would continue to remain with her, once she'd completed her sentence.

'The outcome certainly fits the crime,' Holmes remarked. 'Lady justice has had her day.'

'Indeed. What do you imagine will happen to Langsdale House now?'

Holmes shrugged. 'It has a grim history. No doubt it will sell cheaply enough. Perhaps the next person will do something better with it than the previous owners did?'

'One can hope. And Mulgrave? Will we see him in the dock?'

Holmes shook his head. 'Unlikely. With all we know of this brothel business, including Simpson's testimony, Mulgrave's involvement still cannot be adequately proven. He will not survive an internal investigation, but that is about the best we can hope for. Sergeant Birch gave enough evidence to ensure Mulgrave's dismissal. It will come with heavy financial cost, since it is probable that he will lose any pension available to him on the occasion of his retirement.'

'That is the least they should do. Mulgrave should be in prison, with all the others.'

'I agree with you, but this is the world we live in. Policeman are harder to prosecute, especially senior ones with friends. Still, Sergeant Birch, I'm happy to report, is now Inspector Birch. A gift from the superintendent. His promotion comes with a significant boost to his pension.'

'That does please me,' I said. I continued scribbling my notes on the case. When I looked up, Holmes pointed to my notebook.

'Another for your chronicles, I take it?'

I nodded. 'I was just about to write a title. Do you have a suggestion?'

Holmes thought for a moment.

'Perhaps something less ostentatious this time? How about the Mystery of Langsdale House?'

It was a good title and I thought hard about it.

'I think I shall go with the Langsdale House Mystery instead.'

'Making the house the enigma, eh, Watson? Well, I think you probably have it right.'

THE END

* * * * *

PROGENITOR

BONUS
FIRST TWO CHAPTERS

Chapter One

Friday, August 14, 1942

Washington's sky was on fire...

The car carrying General William Marshall, Chief of Staff of the Army and a member of a new body of joint chiefs established by President Roosevelt, skidded to a halt at the side of the road. General Marshall, and his aide Captain John Keeney, stepped out and surveyed the ruins of the capital in shocked silence.

Plumes of black-grey smoke rose from destroyed historic buildings, feeding a heavy cloud that was choking the light from the city. The engulfing fires below gave the thick sky an ominous glow. Streets, usually busy with traffic, were littered with the rubble of collapsed buildings. Cars stood abandoned where they'd stopped. The intense heat sporadically caught the plumes alight, causing bright flashes and thunder-like rumbles, which turned the sky bright orange. In between those volatile periods of fiery activity, the city became eerily silent, broken only by occasional unrecognisable animal-like noises reverberating through the streets below.

There were no other sounds.

There were no people.

Marshall blinked as the heat and smoke particles washed over him. His face was a roadmap to the ravages of time, and his deep lines and heavy crow's-feet suggested the battle with time was over and he'd lost. Falling ash clung to his close-cropped white hair, and the reddish hue of his age-mottled skin deepened in colour, as he stood watching the sky burn. An acrid odour travelled along the wind. Marshall wiped his blue-grey eyes as the heat induced them to water. He observed Captain Keeney, who leant into the car and turned on the radio. Keeney was a handsome young man in his late twenties, dependable with an excellent grasp of routine that paired well with being an aide to an old forgetful general.

Keeney tuned the radio until a panicked voice cut through the static.

'Turn that up,' General Marshall ordered

'... *it's difficult to make out. There's gunfire, explosions. We're not sure where it's coming from. There are people running in the streets with what looks like animals chasing them. We're just hearing. Hold on. We're hearing that they've attacked the Pentagon. We... We don't know any... Wait, what was that? The building is shaking. There's something in here with us...*'

Marshall fell back against the car. 'The Pentagon?'

Keeney stared into the horizon. 'Bobby,' he muttered.

'Did you hear me? I said turn that up.'

He came back to his senses and adjusted the volume. Muffled screaming replaced the voice, then the station stopped broadcasting.

The young captain found another.

'... *and that's it, stay indoors, barricade yourselves and... wait, what's that? There's something... fuck! The building is shaking, there's something outside... Jesus Christ, what is that? Get out, get out...*'

Marshall looked grim as the voice on the radio gave a hideous scream, and then that station too went dead.

'Are we under attack, General?'

'It looks like it.' General Marshall scanned the street.

'The Germans?'

Marshall's eyes stared unfocused on the heat haze coming from the horizon. 'Could be, or their allies. Hard to believe they made it this far without alerting someone.'

'Where should we go?'

'Let's find a way through and get to the White House,' he said, getting back in the car. 'See if you can find the emergency channel on the radio.'

Captain Keeney spun the wheel and hit the gas. The car jerked at speed, throwing Marshall into the door. He grunted.

'*... homes, barricade yourselves in and wait for further instructions. This is a public service announcement. Stay in your homes, barricade yourselves in and wait for further instructions. This is a public...*'

'Shut it off,' Marshall said.

The car turned into a street and Marshall yelled in warning as chunks of concrete, twisted metal, and glass fell on the road ahead.

'Fuck,' Keeney shouted, shifting into reverse.

Marshall looked behind. 'You're clear.'

Keeney spun the wheel, but the car gave a violent jolt. Marshall's head hit the passenger window, cracking it, and he blacked out.

When General Marshall awoke, he was being dragged along the road. He looked up at Keeney's bloody face and saw his aide's relief. The car was aflame, lying on its side. Keeney helped Marshall up and they both limped away, finding shelter behind a colossal piece of fallen building.

'Are you okay, John?' he asked. His aide nodded.

Marshall was nauseous and dizzy. Rubbing his temple and feeling the wetness there, he looked at his hand and grimaced. It was red with blood. Keeney tore his shirt sleeve, folded it, and wiped Marshall's face.

'What happened?'

'No idea. Something hit us side on. By the time I got out, there was nothing around.'

'Something? Ouch.'

Marshall pushed Keeney away, but the young captain slapped his hand. 'Let me look. You got glass in here.' Keeney removed the visible shards and went to put the cloth against his wound, but the general snatched it away.

'Was it another vehicle?'

'No, it was more like a…'

'What?'

He narrowed his eyes at Keeney's hesitation. His aide's unblinking eyes just stared at the devastation. Marshall waited for a reply. Keeney's eyes were wide. Panicked. Keeney turned back to him. 'Sorry, I wasn't really paying attention, not until we ended up in the side of that building. Something large knocked the car on its side. General, I don't feel safe. We should find somewhere less exposed.'

Marshall pressed the cloth to his temple and it eased his pain. 'Where do you suggest?'

'Maybe we should head away from the city?'

He shook his head. 'Where are we?'

'I'm not sure. I don't recognise this area. Sorry, I'm not a native.'

'Nor me,' he said standing. 'I'm sure that's Lincoln Park. Look for a street sign.'

They scanned the buildings. Keeney pointed. 'There, Twelfth Street.'

'Good, we'll head to the park.'

'On foot?' Keeney's breathing increased. It was clear the idea frightened him. 'I don't know if that's a good idea, sir.'

'John,' Marshall said, taking his arm, 'look at me.'

His haunted eyes met with the general's.

'We're going to be fine, okay?'

Keeney nodded as a tear fell from his eye. 'Sorry, General. I'm just…' He turned and vomited. 'Fuck,' he said, spitting.

'You feel better?'

'No.' He was shaking.

'Sit for a minute. You're in shock.'

Keeney fell next to him. 'Jesus Christ, I'm a fucking wreck.' His aide leant forward and took in a shuddering breath.

'That's it. Deep breaths. Just keep breathing.'

'Bill,' Keeney's uncustomary use of the general's first name got his attention. 'What happened to all the fucking people?'

'I wondered that too. Maybe they were evacuated? Or perhaps they're hiding?'

'Maybe.'

'How are you feeling?'

Kenney's eyes fell to the road. 'Terrified. Absolutely fucking terrified, and I don't know why. The place is just on fire. What the fuck could do this? Was it a bomb? Wouldn't we have felt or seen an explosion? None of this makes any sense.'

General Marshall put a hand on his shoulder. 'I feel it too. The silence... I wish I had answers, but we won't get any sitting here. Let's not speculate. They evacuated everyone they could, that's my feeling. I don't see any bodies, do you?'

He shook his head.

'We have to move on. On your feet, soldier.'

His lips compressed as he nodded. 'To the park, sir?'

Marshall let go of Keeney and wiped his brow. 'Yes, then we'll take Independence Avenue.'

'To the White House?'

'Feels like the best choice. At least there we might get answers.'

Keeney swallowed as he ran eyes along the road. 'If it's still standing.'

'Let's hope so.'

The sky rumbled and went dark. They watched a thicker cloud cover what little light they had, turning the world dark and shadowed. It came with a chill wind.

'Great.' Keeney sighed. 'Now rain too?'

'That's not a bad thing, especially if the city is on fire.'

'True,' Keeney said as the first drops fell.

Marshall slapped his arm. 'Come on.'

They saw no one as they made their cautious walk. They passed abandoned cars, some still running. Navigating roads covered and blocked by debris from collapsed buildings. Keeney suggested using a car, but as they moved further along the densely packed, rubble-strewn streets, it was obvious they'd be quicker on foot. They scanned roads, and buildings, hoping to find answers to what had happened. The only evidence of any people they saw was an assortment of discarded articles of clothing, and a few children's toys.

After a thirty-minute hike, they'd made it to Third Street and could go no further. The Library of Congress and the buildings opposite were all destroyed, their debris scattered across the streets.

Keeney looked around. 'Which way now?'

Marshall rubbed his chin. 'We can't go that way,' he said looking up Third Street. 'Let's see if we can get to Pennsylvania Avenue.'

Keeney grabbed Marshall's arm and pulled him behind a pile of wreckage.

'What?'

Keeney pointed. 'Look,' he whispered.

Marshall observed several shadowy four-legged creatures skittering across the ruins. One turned unnaturally luminous blue eyes their way. They ducked, then peered back over. Marshall breathed a sigh of relief as it disappeared into the shadows. The thumping of his heart blocked every other sound.

'Did it see us?' Keeney's whispered breath made Marshall jump.

'Jesus, John, I don't know. I hope not.'

'What are they?'

'Dogs, I think.'

He caught Keeney's sceptical look as it deepened into a frown. 'They didn't look like any dogs I've ever seen.'

Marshall's agitation came in an irritated hiss. 'Well maybe they weren't dogs then.' He rubbed the sweat from his eyes and let out a lengthy breath. 'They've gone now.'

'Did you see which way they went?'

'Further into those ruins. I couldn't see much beyond it. Stop asking stupid questions.'

John Keeney rolled onto his back and covered his face with his hands. Marshall regretted his outburst because he could tell Keeney was just scared.

'I'm sorry.'

Keeney took his hands away. 'Don't be. I *am* asking stupid fucking questions.'

'That feeling you had before.'

'The fear?'

He nodded. 'Can you describe it?'

'Like I want to vomit again. It's in my head. A nagging sense of… dread, I guess.'

'That's how I feel. I can't explain why, but I think those creatures are herding us.'

Keeney rolled onto his front and peered out towards the rubble of buildings ahead. In an unlit space, he thought he saw a pair of luminous eyes, but they disappeared.

'I'm going to say something wild.' His voice was low, measured. 'These things aren't natural.'

'No, they're not.'

'Like… I don't know how to explain it without sounding stupid.'

'Just say it.'

'Monsters. From a horror flick.' He had that expectant look, like a child waiting for a scolding.

Marshall continued to stare into the devastated building. 'That doesn't sound stupid at all.'

They remained lying for a while longer. A heavy foreboding filled the air, along with occasional flashes in the distance lighting the sky. A rumble of thunder reverberated through the ominous air.

'We should probably move on,' Marshall said.

Keeney nodded and pushed himself up, but Marshall grabbed his arm and he lowered back down. Before Keeney could speak, Marshall gave a signal to mute.

Something had heightened his senses.

Something felt wrong.

A block of concrete nearby tremored, shaking off loose stones. A low rumble behind them, followed by the sounds of more rubble falling, made them turn. A mound in the ruins ahead was growing in slow, pulsating jerks. Debris and earth pushed out and up, creating a giant hillock. It captivated them. What little light remained seemed to leave as the darkness intensified.

They were unable to take their eyes from it.

Something skittered nearby.

The heaviness of the air was choking.

'It looks like something is pushing from underneath,' whispered Keeney.

'Something large,' Marshall agreed. He made a quick scan of the area and spotted a place they could hide.

'Over there,' he said, pointing, 'let's get underneath that collapsed wall.'

They scrabbled away. Marshall monitored the growing mound while Keeney dug a space for them to squeeze in.

The mass grew larger and larger. Its slow surging pulses got faster and faster until it grew like a giant anthill. Then it stopped.

General Marshall wiped the grit from his eyes. There was no further movement and he took in a breath.

Keeney poked his head out of the hole. 'What's happening?'

'It stopped growing.'

The sound of something falling caused Marshall to look back. A few stones rolled down the hill and bounced off the rubble.

There was no other movement. An eerie quietness lingered in the air.

Marshall was about to say something, when the ground shuddered. They each read the other's fear. The shuddering intensified and the ground heaved. They were quickly covered in dust.

A rumbling burst of thunder overhead brought with it a deluge of rain, which soaked them. Marshall helped empty the water filling the hole Keeney had dug for them, which was turning into a muddy pit in the torrential rain. A snuffling alerted them to something nearby.

Marshall put a finger to his lips.

Water ran down their faces, into their eyes and ears, but they didn't move. Marshall pointed up, then into the muddy hole. Keeney understood and shuffled in, Marshall squeezing in beside him. They kept their breathing quiet as they heard movement above. General Marshall pulled out his sidearm. The feel of it seemed to comfort him.

A low growl overhead made them freeze. Then, without warning, the ground heaved and lurched from what might have been an explosion nearby. Debris rained down along with dust that turned to mud in the rain.

They waited for a long time before Marshall poked out his head.

'What do you see?'

'The mound is gone. It's a crater now.'

'It exploded?'

'I think so.'

Something in the pit's core stirred. A horrible dread rose from the pits of their stomach into their shaking hands. Marshall could only stare at the monstrous creature awkwardly heaving itself out of its muddy crater. The general inwardly cursed. He'd spent years rejecting religion and its dogma, which was all undone by his first thought, that a demon was escaping from Hell.

The incubus came to full height. Its body a mixture of molten lava and blackened rocks or scales. As it stretched, vast wings unfurled and flapped. Four armoured arms unfolded and lifted and its long-clawed hands flexed. The monster gave off a misty aura as rain turned to steam against the hideous magma of its body. Four giant bug-like eyes opened, burning with blue fire, and its bulbous, blackened horned head lifted towards the sky. An enormous mouth thundered a chorus of hideous screeching and deep roars, and they covered their ears. The monster's first steps shook the ground, causing bigger debris to fall. The power of its thumped footfalls caused foundation-undermined buildings nearby to collapse further.

Marshall caught sight of yipping black doglike creatures as they joined the larger monster from the shadows. It pushed a path away, taking with it the foreboding terrors that had incapacitated them. It didn't take long for them to come to their senses.

In a slow thumping march, it bellowed an unnatural deafening call. In the distance they heard similar in reply. Everything it touched turned to fire.

Both men exchanged glances, but said nothing.

When the creature was a distance away, they emerged from their muddy hiding place. Marshall gave a furtive look, then tugged at Keeney's sleeve, and they made their escape by slipping and sliding down banks of rubble towards the road. The general glanced back at the massive creature as it made a slow plod through ruined buildings, with more than half of it towering above the buildings it had wandered behind. The question of how Washington had been so quickly destroyed was now answered.

Flashes of intense fire billowed from its gigantic head. Not long after, others joined it.

Marshall and Keeney made it towards another mound and ducked down, as they caught sight of yet another giant monster. It appeared to be heading toward the White House. Marshall turned to Keeney and noticed something wrong. He was lying on his back in the mud, his eyes staring at the sky.

'John?' Marshall shook him, but he was unresponsive.

John Keeney could hear yelling, but the voice was far away. His fear had been too much and his body put him into a safe place. A small part of his mind that had been through years of drilling, compelling him to obey orders, fought against the paralysis. He'd experienced this a few times before in his life. Once, when he was nine or ten, he'd been on a hiking trip with his family in Mexico. He'd woken in bed feeling something moving on his leg. When he threw off the covers, the biggest spider he'd ever seen was making a slow crawl along his thigh towards his crotch. He'd got out a strangled whimper before freezing in terror. Fortunately, his father heard the odd sound and recognised something was wrong. In an instant, he'd smacked the thing across the room and smashed it with his shoe. It was so large it took effort to kill. Keeney remained paralysed for some time after. Neither his mother nor father could reach him.

'John, get up.'

Marshall slapped his face. Keeney's eyes focused. Then he flipped and yelled and his eyes rolled into his head as his body convulsed. Marshall held his head as he shook, willing him to stop, to come out of it. A moment or two passed and the tremors slowed. Keeney closed his eyes and his body relaxed. With no choice, Marshall sat and waited for Keeney to wake. It seemed to take forever, but when he opened his eyes and focused them, the general gave a sigh.

'Welcome back,' he said.

'General?' His speech slurred and his expression was a mix of confusion and disorientation.

'Take a moment. Get your bearings,' Marshall said, as he scanned the area.

Keeney pushed himself up on his elbows. 'What happened…'

'You had a seizure.'

He read the concern in Marshall's eyes.

'Do you have epilepsy, John?'

He looked down. 'When I was a boy.'

'I see. Was it frequent?'

'Occasional. I haven't had an episode—'

'Can you move yet?' Marshall cut him off. 'I'd like to leave.'

'I think so.'

He pushed himself onto his side and with relief, Marshall helped him up.

'We should make for one of those buildings,' Marshall said,

pointing. 'They look stable. Come on.'

'Anything to get out of this rain.'

Together they climbed, then slid down banks of muddy rubble onto a path. They crouch-ran toward the ruined building and, under the overhang of concrete, escaped the onslaught of the unrelenting rain.

As they ventured closer, a low voice came from out of the darkness.

'Get inside, quickly.'

It was a British voice. It startled them at first, but they soon obeyed.

In the darkness a huddled group of weary, scared men and women stared as they walked by. A mixture of military and civilians. Out of the shadow came the source of the voice, and it was someone Marshall recognised. For the first time since he and Keeney had stopped the car, he found a smile.

'Bill?' Colonel Charles Bradley said in surprise. 'My dear fellow, I'm so happy to see you.'

Despite being head to toe in mud, they embraced.

'Braders,' he said, pulling away and looking at him. 'I've never been so pleased to see anyone in my life.'

The British colonel gave him a lopsided grin, then turned to Keeney. 'Hello, John, rough day, eh?'

'I've had better,' Keeney replied with a sigh.

'Yes, I think we all have. We should be safe for a while. When the big ones come, they sort of wander off and draw all the small ones with them.'

'We saw another a little west of here.'

'There's more than two of them. Let's get you checked out,' he said, and called for a medic.

'I want someone to take care of Captain Keeney first. He needs to rest.'

Keeney opened his mouth and Marshall gave him a look. 'Rest, Captain. That's an order.'

Keeney gave a weary nod and found a place to sit. He lay his hands across his knees and dropped his head onto them.

'Is he okay?' Bradley asked.

Marshall took his arm. 'He had a seizure.'

'Why do I get the impression you're not happy about it?'

'A discussion for another time. Have you someone who can look at him?'

When the medic arrived, Colonel Bradley pointed at Keeney. 'See to him, Doc.'

General Marshall turned his back on Captain Keeney and walked away. Colonel Bradley frowned as he looked between them, then followed.

Colonel Bradley was a tall, lean man in his mid-forties. A decorated member of British intelligence and a veteran of high-profile engagements throughout the war. They'd met six months back at an Allied briefing, and the two became friends soon after. The head of intelligence told him Colonel Bradley was a member of the British Joint Intelligence Committee, their highest intelligence body, but when Marshall asked him Charlie laughed at the suggestion. As their friendship deepened, he realised with a man like Charlie – or Braders as he preferred – you'd never know his full story.

They sat together chatting for a while, then Doc arrived and offered them his flask. 'It's not the good stuff,' he said.

Marshall took a swig and was grateful. 'Best I've tasted today.'

The medic ran expert fingers over the general's head and found the wound he'd sustained earlier. 'This wound needs a clean.'

Marshall took another drink and offered the flask back, but the medic shook his head. 'Keep it, sir.'

While the medic continued to clean Marshall's wound, the general looked to his old friend.

'Braders, tell me you know what's going on?'

Despite Bradley's casual manner, Marshall knew him well enough to see the events of the day had taken their toll. 'I think you already know the answer to that, old boy. I had my eye on you both for a while, although I didn't know it was you until just now. When that beast surfaced, we had no choice but to wait. It's one of maybe fifty we've seen today. And you know there's nothing like it on Earth, don't you?'

Marshall grunted as the medic continued his treatment. 'John said the smaller creatures were like something out of a horror flick.'

'Not a poor description, is it?'

'What do you think we're dealing with?'

'Demons? Aliens? Who knows?'

'Demons?' Marshall frowned. 'Talk sense.'

Bradley laughed. 'Extra-terrestrial life is an easier concept for you to believe in?'

'Seems more plausible than supernatural beings from Hell.'

'I won't argue with you. I can't say I'm thrilled with the prospect of Hell on Earth, yet it does seem that way. Supernatural or otherwise.'

'True. We caught a few things on the radio before it went dead. Scraps, really. We didn't see any people on our journey. Are they all dead?'

'Not all of them. They herded most away. Initially, those who hadn't escaped tried to fight, but it was futile. There wasn't time to even form a resistance. Several human-looking creatures began herding people away.'

'Where?'

'No idea. I found what people I could and we've been moving ever since.'

Marshall took another sip. It warmed him. 'How did it start?'

'Quickly. Those giants came out of the earth and in a matter of hours turned Washington into what you see now. While this was going on, these gangly armed oblong-headed things emerged from the pits the larger creatures left behind. They herded people into the streets. They're weak. Bullets put them down easy enough... but the smaller creatures? One man called them monkey-dogs, difficult to spot, unless they're on top of you... and once they are? Well... that's it, I'm afraid.'

'We saw those too.'

Bradley rubbed the bridge of his nose. 'People found out pretty quickly bullets didn't stop them. Nothing apparently does.'

'Have you heard from anyone in the White House?'

'Given what I've seen, I have no reason to expect anyone survived. If they did, I'd imagine they suffered the same fate as everyone else. The White House, like most of the buildings, is an enormous pile of rubble now.'

General Marshall lowered his eyes. 'I don't suppose you know if the president got out alive?'

Colonel Bradley shrugged. 'Maybe. They have contingencies for attacks. There was a lot of activity near the harbour. Happy to report several boats got away. I also imagine the navy got their fleet out. I think it's safe to assume, at least for now, you're the man in charge.'

'I'm glad to have you with me.'

Bradley stood. 'Let's see if we can't find you and John some dry clothes.'

'I feel terrible asking, but… do you have anything to eat?'

He nodded. 'We have supplies, and hot food.'

General Marshall smiled, then winced as the medic dabbed something cold into the cuts on his face. Just like the news he'd got from Colonel Bradley, it hurt like hell.

Chapter Two
Thursday, September 3, 1942

Ten Miles North of Washington, D.C.

Mud erupted with a deafening thunder, showering everyone with slurry and rock. Hearing impaired by a high-pitch whistle, and blinded by stone chips, General Marshall staggered into the arms of another. Someone shouted. The air filled with rapid gunfire. He shook his head and tried to clear his blindness. The world focused into a watery haze as his eyes stared at an unnatural blackness above. Marshall was vaguely aware of someone tugging at him. A massive burst of mud and debris flew into the air, covering them all. He watched as the people around him faltered. Forming a protective barrier in front of him. Marshall swallowed as a hellish thing made from rock and fire heaved itself out of a crater. It roared its indignance as the bright flashes of rockets impacted off its monstrous body. His fear turned to surprise. They'd pushed it back just a little. He felt their emboldened enthusiasm as they pushed forward, but that euphoria left when the monster thumped a giant hand into the earth, rocking the ground and knocking down those who were too close. The enormous disjointed hand then grabbed for those scrabbling away. It found one. Marshall cursed as the terrified kicking and screaming man disappeared into a blackened mouth. He couldn't take his eyes off the poor fellow as the monster's hideous teeth bit down. It threw the remains into a small group, knocking them down as if they were bowling pins, covering them in blood and entrails.

General Marshall yelled for them to fall back. Even though he couldn't hear it he knew they had acknowledged his command, because those he could see turned and ran towards him. The daze Marshall felt cleared, even if his hearing hadn't. Other hands joined those pulling him, as the ground continued to shake. They dumped him into a trench next to others, knocking the air from him, and more soon followed. He blinked at the concerned face of the medic they called Doc. Doc was saying something, but the ringing in Marshall's ears hadn't eased enough for him to understand the words. The sounds of the battle then burst into his head and he could hear Doc's words more clearly.

Doc waved a light in his eyes and Marshall pushed it away. 'I'm alive.'

'General?'

He coughed. 'What's left of him, Doc.'

Doc relaxed. 'You had me worried for a minute,' he said, helping Marshall up.

Marshall took the water bottle offered and drank. He caught sight of his distorted reflection in the door mirror of the transport. His white hair matted with mud and blood.

The air filled with a horrifying screeching roar. They covered their ears.

'Pull the men back, now.'

They called a retreat. Those still attempting to fight were swift to respond.

General Marshall counted as the men funnelled passed, cursing at how few returned. Colonel Bradley approached. His fatigued face thick with mud and sweat.

'That monster's half out. Nothing we've hit it with has any effect.'

Marshall nodded. 'Do we have any artillery munition left?'

Bradley shook his head. 'Bill, it's time to go.'

Marshall cursed. He looked back at the monster and sighed. 'Take what vehicles we can and get everyone to the safety zone.'

'We only have three fuelled.'

'I hate to leave anything behind, but we have no choice. At least tell me we secured the supplies?'

Despite their dire predicament, and his fatigue, Bradley grinned. 'John found what we needed. He's heading back to HQ now.'

Another bellowed roar came and the ground shook as the hideous beast heaved itself fully out from its pit.

'Okay then, time to go,' Marshall said.

Colonel Bradley began issuing commands.

Marshall was the last to enter the troop carrier. He stared back at the monster as the vehicle flew away. It stood taller than the church it had emerged beside. Huge wings unfurled and its blackened body burst alight in orange-blue flames. When it roared into the sky, the same fire erupted from its mouth. It stomped toward them, but soon lost interest as their transports headed away. Marshall pulled the blanket tighter around him and scanned the faces of his frightened men. He smiled but, despite his best effort, they didn't seem very encouraged.

An hour later the vehicles pulled into the old factory compound they'd set as their HQ, and a group of men closed and locked a set of heavy iron gates. The general exited and dropped to the ground, helping tired, demoralised men to disembark. There was a foreboding blanket of darkness where the sun should have been, and Marshall gave a weary sigh as he rubbed his eyes.

'General?'

He looked up as Captain Keeney joined him. 'A real clusterfuck, huh?'

Marshall waited until the last of the men passed him. 'We've had better days, Captain.'

Keeney nodded.

'How'd we do with the supply run?'

'We emptied as many stores as we could. It's a good haul.'

'Tell me there's bourbon?'

'There is. A few cases.'

Marshall found a smile. 'Good. I want to talk to the men. Have them assembled in the church and bring a few bottles with you.'

'Into God's house?' He seemed to disapprove.

'If God has a problem with it, Captain,' – he poked Keeney in the chest – 'let him come and tell me Himself.'

'I'm sorry, sir, I didn't mean…'

'Dismissed, Captain.'

Keeney came to attention and saluted, then turned away.

The general thrust his hands into his pockets and made a slow march to the church. As he passed the front of the trucks, Colonel Bradley joined him.

'You're still mad at him?'

Marshall gave him a sideways look. 'I said it was a discussion for another time.'

Colonel Bradley stopped him. 'Now would seem a good time.' Marshall couldn't miss the edge in his voice. It was out of character and not something the general was used to.

'I value your experience and input, Braders. The issue I have with Keeney isn't open for conversation.'

'I've known you too long, Bill. Harbouring this… grudge? That isn't your style, and it's also pointless given our situation.'

'Colonel, you're crossing a line.'

'Fine. You want this formal? I don't work for you, General. I've tagged along because it suits my interests.' His tone was icy. 'The poor boy is depressed and drinking himself to sleep at night. Whatever the issue is needs fixing. Or we might wake up one morning and find him dead.'

'You're being ridiculous.'

Colonel Bradley laughed. 'I am?'

Marshalled growled. 'Okay, fine. He lied.'

'About what?'

'About his epilepsy.'

Bradley stared at him. 'So?'

General Marshall's face turned red. 'You're right. I'm angry. No… I'm furious. Not disclosing that information put people's lives at risk. Put my life at risk. How can I trust him to lead others into dangerous situations knowing he might have another seizure at any moment? He's a ticking time bomb.'

'You're not wrong. Still…'

'Respectfully, old friend. Please drop it.' Marshall walked away.

They remained silent as they passed a number of men working on vehicles. Marshall glanced at Bradley; a sigh slipped through his lips. 'John's drinking?'

Bradley nodded. 'Heavily.'

'Monitor it, please.'

'As you wish.'

The general touched his shoulder. 'Thank you.'

Bradley then said, 'All this talk of drinking is making me thirsty.'

Marshall smiled. 'Same.'

'We're safe for now. Time to kick off our shoes and relax.'

Marshall chuckled. 'Don't you ever feel the burden of misery?'

'Rarely,' Bradley said. 'At least, not that I show.'

'That British optimism of yours is gonna wear thin after a while.'

'Stiff upper lip and all that? But you might be right.' He gave a heavy sigh. 'Today's encounter was another reminder of how dangerous things have got. I'd hoped, the further away we moved from the city, we'd see less of these monsters.'

Marshall clasped his hands behind his back. 'They must have weaknesses.'

'You're right, but nothing we've tried seems to make a bloody difference.' Bradley ran a hand through his mouse-coloured hair. 'What's our next move?'

'We can't fight these things, and we're wasting munitions and men trying.'

'We're moving on again, then?'

Marshall glanced at him. 'Do we have a choice?'

'I suppose not,' Bradley said. 'We should consider our strategy. It's clear we need better intelligence if we're to win this war.'

'Intelligence? Gathered from where?' Marshall asked, frowning.

'You'd be surprised at what I can dig up.'

Marshall smirked, despite his mood. 'I believe you. But be realistic. We lost the war.'

They reached the side entrance to the church, and Marshall stopped. 'Braders, listen. We've no defence against these monsters and no way of predicting when or where the damn things might come at us. I'm tired of losing.'

Bradley met his gaze. 'Fair point. We should consider heading north.'

'It is less populated.'

Colonel Bradley nodded. 'Assuming these things are only interested in cities, we might see fewer in open country.'

'So, we're agreed?'

Bradley nodded.

'You were right,' Marshall said. 'This is a war, but we're not fighting these monsters because we can't.'

'What are we fighting for, Bill?'

'Our lives.'

General Marshall stepped onto the platform and stood underneath the giant cross of Christ. The room was awash with murmured conversation. Colonel Bradley and Captain Keeney stood to one side. Marshall clasped his hands behind his back as he paced. There were maybe fifty men seated. He remembered when the murmuring would have been difficult to speak above. Not anymore.

'We learned more about these creatures today,' he said. 'Nothing we've tried affects them and our weapons are useless.'

The room was silent. He gave a lengthy pause. 'I had a clear strategy for the fight, but...' He paused to look at dirty weary faces. 'It's time we accept the truth. We've lost.'

The murmuring began and Marshall put up a hand. 'Sixteen men died today. Sixteen.' The room was silent. 'We've moved from town to town. Each time we settle, they come. We've seen our countrymen herded like cattle and taken off to god knows where.'

He paused, then chuckled. 'Not much of a rousing speech, huh? I guess you already know I'm not too good with words.'

A few laughs filtered through the men.

'We've had our share of horrors. We miss our friends, our families. These monsters have taken away our freedom, and we fight daily for what little we can maintain. But it's not enough, and I think you know it. There's only one thing left to do. Survive. I know you were hoping this would be our last move, but we can't stay. You gave oaths when you joined the service, to protect this country. I gave that oath too.' He turned to Captain Keeney, who dropped a box onto the stage.

'The sad truth is, right now, we can't protect it. I'm proud of each one of you. Tomorrow we're going to head north. Before we do so, it's time to make new oaths together.' Keeney handed Marshall and Bradley a bottle, and they stepped into a huddle of men, pouring bourbon into cups as they went.

Marshall stood in their midst. 'We swear,' he said, raising his cup, 'to take care of the weak and the helpless. To look out for one another. We swear to survive.'

The murmur wasn't the rousing cheer he'd hoped for.

'We swear,' Bradley said, coming beside Marshall.

'We swear,' Keeney's voice echoed.

One by one they raised their glasses and called out. When the air was no longer filled by rousing oaths, the sombre mood lightened, and then they drank.

'There's plenty of bourbon,' Marshall said. 'Help yourself.'

They shook his hand as he wandered through them. He met up with Bradley and Keeney shortly afterwards.

'Before we move on,' Marshall said, 'I want to gather as many supplies as we can. Split the men into three groups. Rest one, have the other two pack this place up. Rotate them every four hours. John, you rest with group one. Braders, you join group two and I'll be with the third. Questions?'

'Bill,' Bradley said. 'We'll need petrol if we want to get the vehicles running.'

'He means gas,' Keeney said, smirking. 'I might have a solution to that. I scouted gas stations along the town line earlier. I noticed one with an abandoned tanker. It might be full. Even if it's not, we can probably syphon off what's in the pumps and take it with us.'

Marshall smiled. 'First good news I've heard today. Then the priority must be that tanker. Braders, take what mechanics we have and go get it.'

Marshall turned and stepped back into the men.

Bradley turned to Keeney, who met his smile with a scowl. 'I'm going to bed.'

*

An hour later, Colonel Bradley leant against a doorframe watching Keeney, who'd stripped down to his shorts and was sitting cross-legged in bed, staring at a photograph. Lost in thought, he didn't notice Bradley come in. A cigarette dangled precariously from his lips, and a half-full bottle of bourbon lay propped against his leg.

'Penny for them.'

John Keeney looked up through eyes wet with tears. Wiping his nose, he stubbed his cigarette into an ashtray, and with a slight slur, he said, 'Sorry, didn't see, Colonel.'

He made to get out of bed, but Bradley put a hand up and sat on the edge.

'Did you speak with the general?'

'I tried. But he's being stubborn. He's angry with you. You know him better. How long does he usually keep this going?'

'I've never known him to hold a grudge before.'

Colonel Bradley held out his hand. 'Can I see that?'

Keeney handed him the photograph, then opened the bottle beside him and took another swig. Bradley watched him for a moment, then turned his eyes to the faded picture of a man in uniform.

'Brother?'

Keeney pulled the bottle away from his lips, wiping a tear from his nose, and shook his head.

Bradley gave a tight smile, then handed the photograph back. 'Ah,' he said. 'There's a complication.'

Keeney lifted the bottle, but the colonel's hand stopped him. Keeney's expression darkened. 'What? I can't drink now?'

The colonel raised an eyebrow. 'Don't you know it's rude not to offer the bottle?'

Keeney's frown lifted as he passed it over. Bradley took a mouthful, then handed it back.

'The man in the photograph,' Bradley said. 'Army man, eh?'

Keeney nodded. 'An instructor.'

'What's his name?'

'Bobby. Captain Bobby Rogers.'

'How'd you two meet?'

'At school. We joined up when we were eighteen.'

'You were drafted?'

'No. We signed up a few years before that. I wanted to join the navy and go to some exotic place, far from home. But Bobby doesn't do good on boats, so the army it was.' Keeney laughed and fell back into his bed. Bradley observed him. There was always something childlike about John Keeney, but alcohol allowed it to properly surface. They continued to pass the bottle. Bradley took another mouthful, while Keeney continued.

'Then the war started and everything changed. He stayed instructing. I got posted to the Pentagon and thanks to the general, I was able to get Bobby transferred not long after.'

Bradley lit two cigarettes and handed him one. 'So, neither of you have seen any active duty?'

Keeney shook his head. 'What about you? What's your story?'

'Me? There's not much to tell. My father was an influential

man in the British government, so that gave me a bit of an edge in public life. I lost all three of my brothers in the Great War, it killed my parents. They never recovered. I joined the service just as the war ended. Spent time in France and Germany. Learnt a lot about the cultures, languages, sex… all that fun stuff. Moved from one job or another. When the first rumblings of Hitler's rearmament began, I knew we'd be at war soon enough.'

'I was supposed to be sent to Europe, but the general had other plans for me.'

'You were lucky, then.'

Keeney shrugged. 'I don't feel lucky.'

Bradley smiled and stood. 'You probably want to rest?'

'Oh, please,' Keeney said. 'Don't go yet, and I want to hear more about you.'

'You do, do you?' Bradley chuckled.

'Please?'

'Okay then,' Bradley said, sitting back on the bed. 'Before the new war with Germany started. I had the pick of what I wanted to do. Tried a bit of flying and enjoyed that immensely. An RAF pal took me up in his kite. Such a marvellous feeling being up in the sky. Freeing, you know? I had a taste for the thrill of it and I persuaded him to teach me how to fly. Not long after, Britain declared war on Germany, and that ended all the fun stuff. I was soon sent back to France to pick up my old life and moved around quite a lot. Had a few missions here and there which ended in Poland. I was then recalled to blighty and sent here.'

'You've seen a lot of death then?'

'My fair share.'

Keeney's eyes fell. 'I never saw anyone die before today.'

'It's not something you ever really get used to. So, apart from being an aide to an old grumpy general, what else have you done?'

'Like you, I did flight training for a while. I considered switching to the air force once.'

Bradley chuckled. 'What stopped you?'

Keeney laughed. 'I couldn't get my head around all the instruments.' He took another long drink and eyed Bradley. 'Are you a spy? They say you're a spy, but I don't know if I believe it.'

Bradley leant forward. 'I could be. But I wouldn't be a very good one if I told you, would I? D'you have any family?'

Keeney shrugged. 'Not that I know of. I don't speak with my folks anymore.'

'Because of your relationship with Bobby?'

Keeney looked up at Bradley, his face reddened. 'What do you mean?'

Bradley offered him a smile. 'You're a Kentucky boy, aren't you?'

'How'd you know that?'

'I have a good ear for accents. You're surprised your folks didn't approve? Did you think they ever would?'

Keeney's face flushed a deeper red.

'Look, John, I am not judging you.'

Keeney took another drink. Maybe it was the alcohol, or maybe he felt he could trust Bradley with a secret he'd never spoken out loud in his life. 'I thought my mother might, you know, understand. If I could phrase it right. But my father caught us and went crazy.'

Bradley finished his cigarette. 'Religious type?'

'Yeah.'

'Not surprising, really. Kentucky is in the famed bible belt, isn't it?'

'I don't know where that name came from, but it's accurate,' he sighed. 'I wish…'

'That you knew they were alive?'

He shook his head, a tear fell. 'That I knew Bobby was safe.'

'You must really like him then.'

The boyish captain took another swig of the bottle. 'I don't know why I'm telling you this,' he said, trying to sit up but failing.

'Because you're drunk.'

Keeney laughed then some of his rational thoughts filtered through. 'No one knows, you can't tell anyone, promise you won't.'

'Why would I do that?'

Keeney fell back onto his pillow.

'Listen, John. We're all in a bind. We don't have any information. Maybe Bobby's stuck in some god-awful place like this? Isn't that better thinking than' – Keeney was snoring – 'the alternative.' Bradley chuckled. He took the bottle out of Keeney's hand, pulled the blanket over him, then left.

Outside, Bradley approached Sergeant Hawkinson. 'Hawk, do me a favour. Keep an eye on our young captain for me.'

'Is there a problem, Colonel?'

He handed him the almost empty bottle. 'I'm assuming this was full before he started on it?'

*

On a hillock overlooking a destroyed town, General Marshall and Colonel Bradley lay observing a sizeable group of people being led away by a horde of shadowy creatures. They focused through their binoculars on the ragtag group. Men, women, and children trudged defeated under the watchful eyes of larger creatures. Humanoid but not human, they stood at least eight feet tall with oblong heads and long gangly arms. It was by far the largest concentration of them they'd seen.

The sky lightened, if only a little, and because of it there were fewer smaller shadowy creatures. The night was their playtime where they roamed in sizeable groups. During the daylight hours they usually only saw the humanoid creatures, who were slower and easy to kill.

Bradley tapped Marshall's shoulder and pointed. General Marshall trained his glasses on the gigantic monster in the distance. It was a Destroyer. A name they'd assigned to the winged fire-breathing behemoths that tore apart buildings as if they were paper. They'd seen many bursting from underneath the earth. He could just make out the rocky scales along its back, and even through the safety of distance and binoculars, he still felt a strange sense of dread.

'That's the biggest group of people we've seen so far. How many do you think? Two hundred?' Bradley asked.

'Maybe more,' Marshall replied.

'We don't have the manpower to mount a rescue of this size.'

Marshall sighed. 'That's becoming our biggest issue, isn't it?'

'Picking who to liberate?'

Marshall nodded. 'Smaller numbers make for less risk, but I hate to just abandon them.'

The colonel returned to his binoculars. 'I wonder where they take them?'

'And why,' Marshall said.

Colonel Bradley grimaced. 'I don't think I want to know.'

'One thing is obvious. We can't stay here.'

'And there I was thinking we'd finally found a place to settle, at least for a while.'

'It's been almost a month since we lost radio contact with the other military cells. I'd hoped we'd see a military presence here, or something to suggest we were mounting a response, but there's nothing.' Marshall cursed. 'We still don't understand what caused this and what these things are.'

'Demons, according to Father Doyle.'

The general grunted. 'I'm more inclined to look for a less supernatural answer.'

'Me too, but you have to admit, they fit the profile.'

Marshall made no reply.

'I wonder how they subdue the people?' Bradley murmured.

'I wondered that too.'

'We hardly ever see anyone fighting back. I can't believe everyone they grab goes quietly. I wouldn't.'

'Nor would I. Maybe they're just scared. When one of the big ones gets close, it terrifies me.'

'It's got to be something they give off, you know?

Pheromones maybe? I've learnt to suppress fear, yet around them, I get lost in it too.'

'Just another unanswered question in our never-ending list.'

'Where should we go?'

Marshall pulled out a map. 'I've been giving that a lot of thought. We can't stay in the open. It's pointless, we've proved that. About thirty miles northwest of here is a military complex, Camp Detrick. We'll head there.' He folded the map and shoved it back into his jacket pocket.

'I don't know it,' Bradley said, flipping on his back and staring up at the oppressive blanket of clouds.

'I'm not surprised, it's new.'

'Why is that your choice?'

'It's the only complex I know large enough to house the people we have and any we find along the way.'

'Is there any reason to think it's still standing?'

Marshall gave a slight shrug. 'No reason to assume it's destroyed either. It's not like other bases. It's mostly underground.'

One of the gangly creatures made a trilling noise.

Colonel Bradley turned and grunted. 'That's our cue.'

'They're on the move,' Marshall said, wrapping up his binoculars.

'What's the plan? Grab everyone and head to this Detrick?'

'Yes. With the creatures concentrated here we should be able to bypass them with relative ease.'

'It'll only take one to sound an alarm,' Bradley cautioned.

'I don't see we have much of a choice, do you?'

'No.'

'Let's head back then.'

They scrambled down the bank, remaining crouched as they headed to the path leading to the vehicle. When they felt safe and far enough away from anything that might see them, they relaxed and slowed. Bradley waved Marshall down.

Ahead, under a mass of overgrowth, they both saw a familiar patch of unnatural shadow.

'You see it?' Bradley whispered.

Marshall nodded.

'We're too exposed here. Let's get back to the vehicle.'

They crept forward, keeping low, approaching the vehicle on the opposite side to the overgrowth. Bradley kept his eyes focused on the darkness, while Marshall slipped around and inside the driver's side. He waited for the prearranged signal, and Marshall soon gave it.

Bradley pulled out a long tube and nodded.

Marshall started the vehicle.

In the darkness, something stirred.

Colonel Bradley stiffened. A set of blue luminous eyes appeared in the depth of the dark, followed by a huffing growl. Bradley pulled the tape off the flare, which burst alight with a hiss, and threw it into the shadow then jumped in the vehicle. 'Go!'

Marshall hit the gas and spun the wheel and the vehicle sped away.

With a roar the monkey-dog creature flew out of the shadows and landed just short of the vehicle, but blinded by the flare and fearful of the daylight, it soon skittered back into the darkness.

About the Author

Christopher is a Reader's Favorite award winning author of crime, fantasy, science-fiction, and horror.

His Sherlock Holmes stories, published in the Watson Chronicles, have been recognized by readers and peers alike as faithfully authentic to the original Conan Doyle.

Described by New York Times Bestseller Michael Jan Friedman as "an up-and-coming fantasy voice", and compared to Roger Zelazny's best work, Abbott's Songs of the Osirian series of works brings a bold re-telling of Ancient Egyptian mythology. Abbott presents a fresh view of deities we know, such as Horus, Osiris, and Anubis. He weaves the godlike magic through musical poetry, giving these wonderfully tragic and deeply flawed "gods" different perspective, all the while increasing their mysteriousness.

Christopher has published with Crazy8Press, and has written for major media outlets, including ScreenRant.

Info@cdanabbott.com
cdanabbott@gmail.com
and find him online at:
www.facebook.com/cdanabbott
www.twitter.com/cdanabbott
www.instagram.com/cdanabbott
and at his website:
cdanabbott.com

Ancient Egyptian Fantasy

"In his Songs of the Osirian series, Christopher D. Abbott has reinterpreted Egyptian mythology, creating a moving chessboard of gods, demigods, monsters, and men that is by turns alien and familiar--but always exciting. Abbott's armies assail mighty fortresses. His heroes brave benighted landscapes. His lovers endure terrible hardships. And all the while, the shadow of the reborn Beast grows longer and longer, threatening to engulf all of creation.

If you like epic tales of love and hate, loyalty and betrayal, vengeance and forgiveness...if you like chronicles of Good versus Evil, with the highest prize hanging in the balance...you owe it to yourself to read Songs of the Osirian."

Michael Jan Friedman
New York Times Bestselling Author

Available on Amazon & Barns & Noble

Sci-Fi - Horror

More To Fear Than Fear Itself

When a horde of towering creatures wreaks havoc on FDR's Washington D.C., no one–including the president–knows where they came from. A desperate group of survivors makes it to Fort Detrick, where they seek refuge from the devastation. They think they're safe there. After all, It's FDR's state-of-the-art maximum-security facility. But relief turns to horror, as they find they've locked themselves in with a more hideous threat than the one they left behind.

CRAZY 8 PRESS

crazy8press.com

The Watson Chronicles

Lieutenant Wilson is found dead at Reardon House, Dartford Kent.

But was it a suicide or a murder?

When Inspector Hargreaves of the Kent Constabulary seeks Sherlock Holmes' aid in uncovering the truth, Holmes and Watson become embroiled in an investigation leading to the heart of Westminster. Possibly to the Crown Herself. Who is Sir Henry Wilburton? What is his connection to the late Professor Moriarty? Holmes must weave a dangerous path if he is to reach a successful conclusion. But with war a possible outcome of failure, the stakes are as high as they can get.

Available on Amazon & Barns & Noble

The Watson Chronicles

A mysterious theft at the British Museum is followed by an unexpected death at an archaeology dig in Egypt.

Holmes and Watson follow clues that lead from London to the ancient deserts of Cairo. Exactly who are the Cult of the Free? And what connects them to each event? It falls upon Sherlock Holmes and his faithful friend, Dr Watson, to determine the motives. But it soon becomes apparent that the clues are almost as difficult to discover as the ancient tombs themselves...

Available on Amazon & Barns & Noble

The Watson Chronicles

When Inspector Lestrade discovers a body holding an envelope addressed to Sherlock Holmes, the Scotland Yarder calls the famous detective in for help.

Maurice Harriman died several days earlier under mysterious circumstances. Until his discovery by Lestrade, the body had been resting peacefully in the morgue. When Holmes opens the letter, he discovers an ace of diamonds Black Lantern playing card. Holmes reveals he received the exact card in the post, three days previously. It falls to Holmes and Watson to discover what connects these playing cards with Harriman's death. The case takes a sharp turn when a second card arrives—this time the two of diamonds...

Available on Amazon & Barns & Noble

Printed in Great Britain
by Amazon

86619427R00102